SECRET EMPIRE

BRI BLACKWOOD

BRETAGEY PRESS

Copyright © 2021 by Bri Blackwood

This is a work of fiction. Names, characters, places, and incidents either are the product of the author's imagination or are used fictitiously. Any resemblance to actual persons, living or dead, events, or locales is entirely coincidental. For more information, contact Bri Blackwood.

No part of this book may be reproduced in any form or by any electronic or mechanical means, including information storage and retrieval systems, without written permission from the author, except for the use of brief quotations in a book review.

The subject matter is not appropriate for minors. Please note this novel contains sexual situations, violence, sensitive and offensive language, and dark themes. It also has situations that are dubious and could be triggering.

First Digital Edition: September 2021

Cover Designed by Amanda Walker PA and Design

❀ Created with Vellum

NOTE FROM THE AUTHOR

Hello!

Thank you for taking the time to read this book. Secret Empire is a dark billionaire romance. It is not recommended for minors because it contains adult situations that are dubious, references to sexual abuse and could be triggering. It is a standalone and the book ends with a happily ever after for our couple.

It would be helpful for you to read Savage Empire, Scarred Empire, Steel Empire, and Shadow Empire before reading this book. The next book in the series is Stolen Empire.

BLURB

Forbidden moments and secrets...

She ran and hid in one of the biggest cities in the world.

It's the best place to remain anonymous if you try hard enough.

But that all comes crashing down when I spend the night with her.

My new assistant.

I made a vow to never mention the night we spent together again.

She didn't know who I was and I preferred to keep it that way.

But when her past comes back to haunt her

I'm the only one who can help her fight the demons that curse her.

PLAYLIST

Met Him Last Night - Demi Lovato and Ariana Grande
Reckless. - JoJo
NDA - Billie Eilish
Carless Whisper - Seether
Toxic - Britney Spears
Marry The Night - Lady Gaga
Sweet Child O' Mine - Guns N' Roses
Broken & Beautiful - Kelly Clarkson
Reflection (2020) - Christina Aguilera
STAY - The Kid LAROI, Justin Bieber
Rise - Katy Perry
Feeling Good - Chlöe

The playlist can be found on Spotify.

GAGE
FOUR YEARS AGO

Rain erupted from the sky, making an already dreary day even more so, but it did little to hide the events that I watched unfold in front of me. Yes, I was guilty of doing some dirty shit over the years, but the person I couldn't take my eyes off of had done the lowest of the low.

I wasn't shocked by the news. I knew it was only a matter of time before it would happen, yet the result still surprised me.

As the rain picked up, I watched someone who had no business walking these streets roaming free. It made my blood boil because they were let loose because of a so-called 'technicality'. I knew it was bullshit and that someone had greased some hands to make sure that the evidence had disappeared and that the authorities dropped the charges.

There wasn't anything I could do about it.

At least not yet.

It would start a fight that my gut told me would cause devastation that no one was prepared for. The benefits of holding back and biding my time made me wonder if they outweighed the cost.

When the asshole looked in my direction, I hoped they could identify me, so I could see the fear in their eyes when they realized I was watching them. But no sense of recognition crossed their features before they entered the car that would whisk them away, back to the life they experienced before they were arrested. I knew arrangements were already being made so that their life would resume as if nothing had happened. But I wouldn't rest until I took them down.

The damage they'd caused had ruined the lives of many and no one had the power to take them down beside me. But the timing wasn't right.

So, for now, all I could do was watch from the sidelines until it was time to strike. Because when the time was right, things would happen quickly and when this was over, I promised that this would all end and they would pay for what they'd done.

But there were two larger questions that remained: Who'd sprung this person loose and why?

1

MELISSA
FOUR YEARS AGO

Before I walked around the corner, I took a deep breath to calm myself. It could have been because of nerves, or because I just ran up several flights of stairs to get here, but my heart was racing. I took several more deep breaths, rubbed my slightly sweaty hands on my jeans, and then continued on my way.

"Ms. Davis?" I asked as I knocked on the open door, still somewhat breathless. The woman in question stopped typing on her computer and looked up at me with a smile on her face.

"Melissa, please sit down. I'm glad you were able to make time to meet with me today. This shouldn't take too long."

I sat down in a chair in front of her desk. "It was no problem. Your office is on my way to class anyway."

Her smile eased some of the stress I'd been feeling. It didn't seem as if she'd asked me to meet her about something bad. If it had, that would be the last thing I needed. It was the spring of my senior year at NYU, and I was growing nervous about what I would do after I graduated. There was no way I was going back to Ohio, having grown fond of New York City, the place I'd called home since I was eighteen. But with graduation looming and me not having any idea what I was going to be doing after, I'd been stressed to the max on top of everything I needed to do to wrap up my courses.

"Are you okay?"

I guess the stress I was feeling was easy to read, but that wasn't shocking. I'd come to her often to discuss what I would be doing after I graduated. "Just stressed about, well, everything."

Ms. Davis smiled again. "There's nothing you need to worry about, Melissa. You are one of the best students I've come across during my time here."

A surge of pride filled me. I'd done everything in my power to excel here. In part, I was highly driven by the desire to not go back home. "Yeah, but I don't have any plans after graduation yet."

"That's what I wanted to talk to you about. This came across my desk, and I thought you might be interested in applying for the job."

I quickly scanned the paper before looking up at her. The information in front of me was a detailed job description. I should have been happy, but I was dejected over the document in front of me. "I never intended on being someone's assistant. I want to go into business."

Ms. Davis nodded. "I know that but let me let you in on a little secret. Have you heard of Cross Industries?"

I scoffed. "Of course I have. They are one of the biggest companies in the world and I—" I stopped speaking as she slightly leaned in before glancing at the sheet that she handed me. "No way."

This was a position with Cross Industries? If you didn't know about that company, you had to be living under a rock. During my search to figure out if I should continue with school or look for a job, I'd tried to see if they had any openings at an entry level and couldn't find any. It seemed as if many of the employees stayed around forever due to the culture and benefits they received while working there. I couldn't blame them, but it also made it harder for people like me to even get a shot at working there.

"All I'm saying is that it wouldn't hurt to apply for this job and see where it takes you. I'll keep recommending jobs to you if I see any openings, but this came across my desk and I thought I would share it with you."

"Thank you. I appreciate this a lot. Let me think about it, but like you said, it wouldn't hurt to apply." I scanned the document again and saw that I met most of the qualifications and that it specifically mentioned that there was an opportunity for growth. If what I heard about Cross Industries was correct, I'd probably have no problem being able to afford living in New York City, and that far outweighed anything else in my mind.

There is no way in hell I would ever go back to Ohio. I'd left everything behind in that place, and I refused to return there. Newham, Ohio could implode for all I cared. I felt as if New York City, my mother's hometown, had adopted me with open arms. If I were able to get this or another job offer, this would be an opportunity for me to make my mark in this world. I wasn't about to give that up.

"Is there anything else you would like to discuss with me?"

I thought about it for a second before I responded. "No. Thanks again."

I stood up, swung my backpack around, and folded the piece of paper so that it fit neatly into the front pocket.

"Feel free to schedule an appointment or send me an email if you need anything."

"Will do. I'm sure I'll be back to see you soon."

Ms. Davis chuckled. "I don't have any problems with that. I want to do anything I can to help you succeed."

Her kind words almost made me emotional, but I held it together. "I feel like a broken record by saying thank you again."

She waved me off. "You should probably get to class."

Before I could thank her again, I waved and walked out of the office. Little did I know, the piece of paper with the job description would be burning a hole in my backpack for the rest of the day.

I SAT on my couch and stared at the piece of paper that I laid next to me once I was finished with classes for the day. My older laptop was out on my lap, and I'd been staring at my résumé for the last twenty minutes as I debated applying for the job.

I tapped my fingers absentmindedly on the corner of my laptop as I thought about all of the possibilities that would be laid out in front of me if I did apply and get this job.

It wasn't the path I saw myself taking, but if it could lead to more opportunities, why shouldn't I at least apply for it? If Ms. Davis was right and this was a job within Cross Industries, just having that company's name on my résumé would open doors for me. Nothing on the piece of paper and the form that I currently had open in my web browser, gave any indication that it was a job with the company, but that could easily be explained because they were using a recruiter to find applicants for the vacancy.

Although I had nothing to lose, I don't know why I had such issues with just writing the cover letter and applying for the job. If I did get selected, I would still be able to choose whether I wanted to take the job.

I rubbed my hands across my face. I was over applying for jobs, even though it was a necessary evil for me. Some of the ones I applied for I'd gotten rejected outright, while others I'd gotten called into interviews, and I had several I was still in the process of interviewing for. Then again, what was one more opportunity that would probably be added to my pile of rejections?

"Screw it," I mumbled to myself as I opened a Word document and started composing a cover letter, in the back of my mind knowing that there was a very high chance that this would be another addition to the trash.

2

MELISSA
EIGHT MONTHS AGO

With a heavy breath I stood up and stretched my body, which had been curled up in a ball for far longer than I thought. The only reason I had gotten up was because my phone rang, and I had left it in my bathroom when I stopped in there to remove my contacts. I picked up the offending object and glanced down at the screen. I shook my head at the name, knowing that nothing good would come of this on a Friday night.

"Hey, Nia."

"Get dressed."

"Wait...why?" I looked down at my ratty T-shirt and sweatpants before looking back at the phone. Nia was one of the few friends I made after I graduated from NYU, and I now debated how long she would stay on that list. I enjoyed having a small circle of friends, but she was skating on thin ice with her latest demand. It didn't help that I was always suspicious about what she might have up her sleeve.

"We're going out."

I couldn't contain my displeasure as I groaned and threw

my head back. I knew nothing good was going to come of this call. "I don't want to."

"You never want to and that changes tonight. So put on your big-girl panties and let's go. It's about time you let loose and have some fun."

"But I don't want to?" This time it came out as more of a question than a statement.

"It won't be your typical bar-hopping extravaganza."

That piqued my interest. "What do you mean?"

"You'll have to come to my place and find out. You have forty-five minutes. Wear a little black dress."

With that, she hung up the phone with a decisive click. I wasn't shocked that she hung up on me because it was a tactic she had used before to get me to do what she wanted. I could just ignore her and go back to watching the movie that Nia had so rudely interrupted. Then again, I wanted to know what she had up her sleeve.

"Why am I even entertaining this?" I mumbled as I stepped out of the bathroom and into my bedroom closet. I flung some of the hangers aside as I looked for one little black dress in particular that I thought would work well tonight. When I found the dress I wanted, I pulled it off the hanger and examined it.

I walked out of the closet and tossed the dress on my bed. I made a mental list, much like one that kept me organized at work, of what I needed to do so that I could get to Nia's apartment in forty-five minutes.

Before I could blink, I was ready to go and grabbed an old bag that Nia would probably judge me for having and walked out of my apartment.

My trip to Nia's was uneventful and I only had to ring the doorbell once before the woman of the hour answered.

"About time you got here."

"I got here within forty-five minutes just like you requested."

Nia waved me off before opening her front door wider so that I could come in. The first thing I noticed was that she was dressed similarly to me, wearing a tight black dress and high heels. The look was perfect for a warm summer's evening out on the town. The biggest difference between the two of us was her striking red hair compared to my mousy brown.

"Whatever. All that matters is that you're here now."

I fought off my impatience that was threatening to show. "And I still have no idea what we're doing."

"We're going to get you laid tonight."

I did a double take. "Excuse me?"

"You didn't mishear me." She took the opportunity to fluff my hair. "Nice touch on going with the darker eyes and lip. Very different from what you usually do."

"Pause. Can we go back to the getting laid part?"

She sighed as if what she told me was the most normal thing in the world. "Everything you need is over there." She pointed to her dining room table, and I warily followed, not trusting what I would find.

On the table sat a gift bag, which made my suspicions intensify. It was clear she wanted to build suspense. I walked over to the bag and without thinking twice about it, pulled out the contents.

"You weren't kidding about the sex thing at all," I said as I glanced at the items. I lifted up the packs of condoms, a blonde wig, and a mask, similar to one you might see at a masquerade ball.

"Nope. Mission Get Melissa St. Hill Laid is in effect for tonight. I bet you've never done anything this wild before. Thought the wig might be a nice addition, but the mask was required."

Little did she know. "You're right. I don't think I have and I'm not too sure I want to do it now."

"I totally get it and if you don't want to do it, that's completely fine. I just know you mentioned being interested in getting out there more and…"

"Nia, this wasn't exactly what I had in mind." That was an understatement. I ran both hands through my hair, probably messing up any effort I'd made in making it look nice.

"I read between the lines, and you want to have a man between your legs, so let's go."

"I don't want—"

Nia took a deep breath. "If you don't want to go, that's fine. No pressure. But I was invited to a party tonight where anything goes."

That made me catch my breath. "Where is this party?"

I wondered if she would say Elevate, the club in town that my boss co-owned with his brothers. I only knew about the establishment due to work and the confidentiality agreements I had signed.

"Oh, it's at someone's house not too far away. A lot of information that I learned about the party was via encrypted text message. I assume it was due to trying to keep things as tight-lipped as possible."

I tried not to let the relief show on my face when she confirmed that the place had nothing to do with Elevate. It would be so awkward to go to that club when there was a high chance of running into your boss.

"What information can you give me about this place?"

"The security there has been top-notch. Outside of my contact I have no idea who will be there, but I was told that everyone went through the rigorous screening process that I went through."

I took a step back from the table. "Wait a minute. If you went through a rigorous screening process in order to get this invitation, how were you able to invite me?" When she didn't respond right away, I closed my eyes and willed myself not to yell at her. "You gave them personal information about me, didn't you?"

Nia grimaced. "Not too much. It wasn't like I had to give them your Social Security number and things like that.... Not that I had that information to give to them anyway."

"It's clear that whoever this is now knows more information about me than I know about them." I groaned, not fully believing the situation she had gotten me in. "Fine. Let's go."

I could tell that my answer shocked her because Nia just stared at me before she reacted. She jumped and clapped her hands, excited that I had agreed to go on this little adventure with her. "I knew you'd like this! This is going to be so much fun."

"Yeah. I'm sure it will be."

"Does my wig look fine?"

Nia glanced at me. "It does, for the fourth time. Stop adjusting it."

I dropped my hands to my side. "I don't know what I was expecting when you told me that this party was taking place at a house, but I wasn't expecting this to be a palace."

Nia chuckled. "It's stunning, isn't it?"

Stunning was an understatement. I was pretty sure I'd only seen grander homes on television. The mansion showcased how wealthy the owners were through the gold, black, and white interior design. The high ceilings and the chandelier we stood under were impeccable. How Nia had gotten invited to such a party was beyond me.

She wasn't kidding about the security either. Our phones were confiscated when we entered, and while I understood the reasoning, it removed that sense of security. What happened if and when Nia and I were separated?

I guessed we would have to figure something out if it came down to it, although I assumed it would be as a result of her trying to have sex with someone versus me.

"See? So, this isn't so bad, right?"

"Well, we only just got here so I haven't had enough time to form an opinion."

"I'm sure you'll have rated this party very highly by the time we leave."

Her response made me suspicious. "What did you do?"

"This time nothing, I swear. I'm just assuming that it won't take long for either of us to find someone based on how we look tonight."

I chuckled, though I had to agree. If there was anything I could say about Nia, it was that she had the confidence that anyone would envy, and if I was going to be here tonight, I hoped some of it rubbed off on me.

"Welcome to my home!"

The loud outburst shocked me, but Nia turned toward the person with a smile.

"Nia, darling, it's so lovely to see you again."

"Likewise. Thanks for inviting me to this party, Kiki. I brought my good friend Melissa with me." Nia glanced at me before turning back to Kiki.

"Lovely to meet you and welcome to my home," she said as she held out her hand for me to shake. When I returned the gesture, I took the opportunity to look at her. It was clear this woman was wealthy and had no problem flaunting it. She had on a negligee under her robe, which I assumed was made from pure silk, or so it felt like when the fabric brushed up against me when we shook hands.

"I have to continue greeting my guests, but if you need anything, feel free to let any of my staff know."

We both gave her polite smiles before she walked up to another group of people with her head held high.

"Staff?"

Nia shook her head in disbelief. "I knew she was loaded, but not this loaded."

"How'd you meet her?"

"She's one of my clients."

That made sense. Nia worked as a personal shopper and had many clients who floated in the upper echelon of New York City society.

"She's interesting."

"You only know half of it."

As we moved farther into the room, I started to gain a sense of belonging that hadn't been there when I first entered the home. A surge of confidence—fake or real, who really knew—flowed through me, making me feel more alive than I'd felt since I first stepped foot in New York City.

"Should we get drinks or something?"

Nia smiled. "Now you're speaking my language."

Once Nia had procured a fruity drink for herself and a beer for me, we stood near one of the corners of the room and watched what was going on around us. As the lights lowered, it was clear to see that the vibe of this party had changed. Out went pleasantries and small talk and in came the touching and groping that I expected when Nia told me what type of party we would be attending. Some were taking it a step further than I was willing to in a public space. Several couples and groups of people were making out in different sections of the large room, and I couldn't deny that it was turning me on. I slightly adjusted my mask and the blonde wig and when I looked to my left, I found that someone was staring back at me.

He was partially shrouded in darkness, but his mask did nothing to hide the danger that lurked beneath.

"You've caught his eye," Nia said, nudging me slightly. "Why don't you go talk to him?"

"Because I don't even know if I want to know where it might lead."

"But you're curious."

That was true. The way he sipped his drink alone was turning me on, and I felt as if the way his eyes danced over my body had to mean that he was too. I licked my lips slightly, enjoying the attention he was bestowing on me.

"Go."

"I can't leave you."

"The whole point of this was for us to get you laid. I'll meet up with you after."

"How? We don't have our phones."

Nia waved me off. "I'll find you, don't worry. Go on and have some fun for once in your life. You've more than earned it."

She pushed me a little, causing me to take a couple of steps involuntarily. His eyes never left me, and I swallowed the slight embarrassment that I felt due to the thoughts I was having and the memories that I envisioned creating with him.

After I took another swig of my beer, I made my way over to him. What was I supposed to say when I reached him? Your everyday typical hello?

The closer I got, the more that was revealed to me. The dark suit he was wearing with a white button-down done up at the collar revealed very little, but it didn't take much for me to notice the way the tailored suit hid a strong, muscular upper body. If I knew anything from working at my job for all of these years, it was that no matter how plain a suit looked, you could tell which ones were expensive by their fit. I couldn't get a sense of what his other features were due to how far away I was from him and how much the mask covered, but when he moved his glass away from his mouth, I could see that he had a strong jaw and lips that would drive any woman wild.

I looked back to see where Nia was and found her standing where I left her, but it seemed that she'd gotten the attention of a man too. At least she'd have her own fun to get up to if she decided that was what she wanted to do.

"Hello."

When I turned back around, the man who had been studying me just a moment ago was standing in front of me and he looked even more imposing up close. I couldn't tell if he was making his voice deeper on purpose and I didn't care. I tucked a piece of the wig behind one ear as his eyes stared into mine. The dark orbs held me under their scrutinizing gaze, determined to break me if given the chance.

"I couldn't help but notice you staring."

"People-watching is a wonderful sport to partake in."

His chuckle caused a rush of warmth to flow through me, and I knew that if I wasn't already wet from just his stare, I was definitely wet now.

"I know something else I enjoy partaking in."

You deserve to have fun. I repeated the mantra in my mind before I asked, "A-and what is that?"

His eyes turned even darker if that was possible. "Why don't I show you instead?"

The huskiness of his voice mixed with how much of his face was hidden because of the mask and the now lack of light in the room was a complete turn-on. I was going to have sex with a stranger and just the thought of it thrilled me. The air shifted as he lifted my head up and stared at my mouth, before his lips took over mine. That rush of warmth that I thought I felt a few seconds before increased tenfold as the kiss deepened. Time ceased to exist as he was the only one who mattered now.

"Come with me. I don't share anything that is mine."

I could feel my face heat up at his words and I was grateful for the dimmed lights. Rational me would have thought that his words were a red flag, but the lust-induced haze that I was under had other plans as I placed my hand in his and followed him to who knows where. In the back of my mind, I hoped this wouldn't lead to me ending up on any crime shows, but if his mouth held any promises as to what the rest of his body could do, I was more than willing to take the chance. Plus, Nia had said that everyone who had been cleared to enter this party had to go through a rigorous process of getting approved.

So, what was the harm?

3
MELISSA

He knocked on another door and the moans that we heard in response told us all we needed to know. The man who was leading me down the dark hallway grunted before continuing, in hopes of finding what I assumed to be an empty place for us to fuck.

I tightened my grip on his hand before he could open the door and he glanced at me over his shoulder.

"Whatever happens here, stays here," I whispered to him. I didn't need this rendezvous to go beyond the walls of this house.

I took his grunt to mean that he agreed, and as soon as he closed the door behind us, he was on me. I didn't know where in the house he'd taken me, but from what I could quickly tell, the room was empty unlike what was behind the doors he'd just knocked on. He maneuvered us around and before I could count to three, I was up against the door. Thoughts of where we were and what we were doing thrilled me. Someone could knock and try to walk in at any minute. My body happened to be blocking the only entrance that I saw unless someone wanted to come in through the window.

He tilted my head up with his fist, and almost immediately my lips were pressed to his.

There was no time for thinking. Only feeling. The lack of conversation between us further fed into my arousal as I came to terms with the fact that I was about to have sex with a man who was a stranger. Never had I been so reckless, I always made sure to live my life within the boundaries I set.

He growled just before he broke our kiss, and his mouth attacked my neck. When I felt the material from his mask lightly touch my skin, I briefly closed my eyes. His mask be damned, I needed more. Wanted more. I kissed him harder, the urgency to find our releases and the potential to get caught raising the stakes.

I moaned as the assault on my neck continued. It only encouraged him to go further. His hand settled on my thigh, and I anticipated where it would eventually land. When it inched in that direction, I moaned, completely and utterly ready for him to take me there.

"Spread 'em." His voice was a harsh whisper and I eagerly complied.

When his fingers were inches away from touching my pussy, I held my breath until he touched my folds before one finger made its way inside of me. He nibbled on my neck when he found my secret: just how wet he'd made me.

My head fell back and hit the door with a small thud and I almost forgot I had a wig on my head that wasn't fastened too tightly. Although it was dark enough in this room, I didn't want it to fall off and give him a hint of what I might look like behind my disguise.

My desire to live a very controlled life since I'd arrived in New York City had been turned on its head. This was the most out of control that I'd felt in a long time.

When he worked two fingers into me, I moaned in delight. My body's natural reaction took over as I began to ride his fingers. He grunted in response, and I took it to mean that he was happy with my decision. I could feel my orgasm building up inside of me and I nearly cursed at myself when my head fell back and hit the door again, risking the loss of my wig.

He seemed none the wiser, groaning just before he pulled his fingers out of me. He took a small step back before I heard some rustling and what sounded like a condom wrapper ripping. When all grew quiet again outside of my heavy breathing, he came closer again and I could just make out his lips in the moonlight before he leaned down to kiss me. This kiss was fueled with more urgency as I felt his cock near my entrance.

What happened next happened almost too quickly for me to comprehend. He confidently lifted me up and instinctively my legs went around his waist. I held my breath as his cock entered me and it all came rushing out of me when he pulled almost all the way out before surging back in. I yelped in response and quickly overcame it as he found his flow. I'd known this was going to be quick, yet I still wasn't prepared.

Fucking against a door was an entirely new experience for me and it was sending shockwaves through my body.

"Fuck, sweetheart."

The term of endearment and the gruffness of his voice when he said it, nearly did me in as he continued to pound into me. I could feel myself getting close as he continued the onslaught of pleasure to my body.

I squealed when he changed up his movements momentarily, but when he went back to claiming my body, I couldn't hold back anymore.

I cried out as my orgasm tore through my body, but even that didn't stop his motions. His thrusting continued and when he'd reached his breaking point, his panting became more harsh and a low roar left his throat as he came.

Everything stopped and all we could do was listen to each other try to catch our breath. He released my legs and allowed me to slowly detach myself from his body until I was standing on my own once more.

"Don't move." Although he whispered the words, the command was loud and clear as he backed away from me, leaving me alone in the room for the first time. I saw a light come on in another room, heard some water running before both were shut off.

The man who'd just turned my world upside down was back in front of me and helped me fix my dress and mask in the moonlight. He stared at me until I nodded, silently communicating that I was ready to go. He grabbed my hand and led me through the long dark hallway.

He walked me to the front door of Kiki's home before he turned to me and said, "Phone number."

"Huh?" I asked before I rattled my number off from memory. I didn't remember what I'd told him about this being a one-night thing until after I said the last digit.

"I'll call you."

I didn't respond, and with that he was gone from my life,

just as quickly as he came into it. I doubted he'd call, but it was a nice passing thought.

"Someone had a lovely time tonight."

I turned to find Nia standing next to me with a smirk firmly planted on her face. "Where did you come from? Don't—"

Nia shook her head. "You don't even have to say a word. I'm happy that you decided to have fun. Now let's go home."

I'D JUST HAD the best sex of my life and I didn't even know his name.

This wasn't something I usually did, especially since coming to New York City, but I couldn't deny the thrill that it gave me.

I closed my door with a resounding thud, but my thoughts refused to waver from what had just occurred.

I walked into my bathroom and snatched the wig and the mask off. I thought about taking it off in the taxi on the way home, but I didn't want the driver to sense what had happened. When I looked at myself in the mirror, my face was lit up as bright as a spotlight and the redness in it did nothing for my complexion. If having fantastic sex was an entry in the dictionary, my picture would be listed right next to it. As I stared at myself, all I could hear was the low rumble of his voice in my ear.

Sweetheart.

I could take that nickname in many ways, but hearing it flow off his lips was an aphrodisiac. The way he said it sounded as if he owned my whole body and soul, although it was just for that moment. Hell, I thought I could surrender to him right now if he was here and I heard him whisper it to me.

Tonight took away the pain for a short period of time.

Shifting my attention, I turned on the shower, determined to remove tonight's events from my skin. I glanced up at the showerhead as the water beat down over me, thankful to be able to afford this living space. If Damien Cross hadn't hired me, I don't know where I would be right now.

You know exactly where you'd be.

My inner thoughts confessed the truth, one that I couldn't deny if I tried.

Once I pulled my hair up, hoping to avoid getting it wet, I stepped into the shower with a sigh, allowing the water to flow around my body. I repeated a mantra that got me through the hard times.

I'm not going back there.

Most times it helped, but tonight was something different. A slight shiver ran down my spine, but I wasn't cold. My shower was ruined because of the memories that continued to haunt me.

I wrapped up my shower and exited much quicker than I intended. When I was out of the bathroom, I double-checked the locks on my door and windows to be safe. Once that was done, I walked into the kitchen and snatched my phone off the countertop before leaning back against it. Although I tried to keep work at work, sometimes staying busy was helpful to keep me from tumbling into thoughts of my past. Or I could spend my time thinking about the adventure that my body had taken tonight.

That would have been lovely, except I knew I would never

see that person again. But damn it if I didn't still hear his voice in my head. I knew he was talking in more hushed tones due to where we were and the event we were attending, but his words still had their intended effect.

I closed my eyes briefly before concentrating on my phone, checking my work email to see if there was anything pressing to attend to. When I found an email from Martin Cross in my inbox, I nearly threw my phone across the room. With a shaky thumb, I opened it.

SUBJECT: *New Assignment*

Hi Melissa,

I've asked my assistant to send you a calendar invite to come and meet with me and Damien on Monday morning. We want to discuss with you a change in your role with the company.

Sincerely,
Martin

WHAT THE HELL?

My thoughts raced at what this could mean. At least it didn't sound as if I was losing my job. That was something I couldn't afford to have happen, nor did I truly want it to. Working for Cross Industries had been mostly a dream. Every job had its ups and downs, but for the most part, my time in this position had been lovely. Plus, I was grateful to Damien and Martin for taking a chance on me, having been young when I applied for the job.

Maybe it was a promotion? That would be wonderful.

Another email came through just as I was closing out of

the one from Martin and without a second thought, I opened it. What I saw made me almost drop my phone on the ground. I had vowed never to open an email from that person again, but I couldn't predict the future. I couldn't believe they'd found me.

My heart raced as I tripped over my feet trying to get to my bedroom. I rushed over to close the curtains before I almost knocked my lamp off of my nightstand in an attempt to turn it on. Once I had more light, I ran into the closet and dug around until I found a small case with a keypad. I typed in the number I knew by heart and flipped open the top. A big breath left my lungs.

Okay. It was still here. Right where I put it.

I closed the top and put the case back in its resting place before begging myself to calm down. I'd had enough excitement for one night.

4
GAGE
SIX MONTHS AGO

I flipped the phone over in my hand once. And then twice. It should be easy to make this phone call, but it wasn't. I couldn't get myself to do it.

It was one of the many burner phones that I had at any given time. All I wanted to do was stare at the device in my hand.

There was another thing I couldn't get out of my mind.

The woman I fucked at Kiki's party. The one who'd distracted me when I was supposed to be tending to a project I'd been working on. And I'd messed up when I went after her, throwing the whole point of why I was there out the window. But I couldn't stop myself because for whatever reason, I felt drawn to her presence. It had little to do with the slinky black dress she'd worn that did a fantastic job of showing off her curves just before the lights were turned down. She'd had my attention the moment she'd entered the room.

This new feeling was strange. I'd had no problem fucking and moving on from past escapades without incident. I made it clear where things stood between me and the women I had sex with. Yet, here I was sitting here thinking about an encounter that happened all too quickly for my liking. I hadn't gotten my proper fill and that pissed me off. My body craved more, and I had a hard time moving on from anything until I got what I wanted.

I'd added her number to the phone that I was flipping between my fingers but hadn't bothered to call. Even though I couldn't get her off my mind, I told myself I wouldn't contact her.

There were plenty of reasons why it was a bad idea. Several priorities had taken over my life, convincing me that I should leave what happened at the party there. I'd found out about the party last minute and it had been almost too easy to score an invitation to it.

It had been years since I'd seen Kiki in person. That had been on purpose, but she never strayed too far from my mind. Kiki had been a friend of my mother's from their college days, and she'd visited the Cross Estate when I was sixteen. She'd come on to me while visiting when she 'made a mistake' and walked into my room naked. She'd had her hands on me when my father burst into the room and threw her out once he told Mom what had happened. I'd never been in the same room with her again until the night I walked into her party.

I shook my head and attempted to get some work done. I picked up some of the papers that were strewn around on my desk, in search of the file that evaded me, before I found myself staring at the burner phone.

Where is my file on Pryce?

Jeff Pryce owned a series of hotels in the tri-state area,

which was an avenue that I wanted to explore. Hell, I might end up buying his properties in the end. This was an exploratory, information-gathering exercise, and I promised myself that I would keep everything aboveboard. At least for now.

A knock on my office door brought me out of my thoughts.

"Come in."

"Mr. Cross, I—"

I immediately tuned my assistant out. Callie had been on the job for maybe two to three months but hadn't been much help. I ended up doing a lot of things myself because even after I explained things to her multiple times, she still hadn't figured out what I wanted. The only reason she still had a job was because Dad had convinced me to give her another chance after he watched her fumble on a project that she was working on for me. I think he was becoming less cutthroat the older he got.

"Mr. Cross?"

Her saying my last name forced my attention back to her. I told her a million times to call me Gage and now that irritated me too. "Did you find the information on Pryce like I asked you to a few days ago?" That had to be the reason why I couldn't find his file.

"That's what I wanted to talk to you about. You see—"

"Is this going to be another excuse?"

She jerked her head back, clearly shocked by my outburst. "I—"

"That was a yes or no question. Do you have the information on Pryce?"

"No."

I sighed. "You're fired."

"What?"

"You're fired. Clear your desk in the next thirty minutes or I'll have security escort you out." I smiled at her, but it was anything but friendly.

With a slight nod of her head, she left my office, closing the door softly behind her. Hopefully she would be able to understand and execute that direction.

Firing her was long overdue; I should have done it earlier. Dealing with her was money and time wasted. There had to be someone more competent who could take her place.

Sometimes, people took my ability to joke around as a sign of weakness, when in fact, they should have been more afraid. I wasn't nearly as lenient or as patient as my two brothers, as Callie had learned the hard way.

I picked up the burner phone again and turned it on. Not shocked to not see any messages or notifications, I quickly found the number I'd been looking for.

The woman in the mask.

I added her number into my personal phone before I could think anything of it. Thoughts of what I'd just done slid from my mind when a muffled ringing could be heard coming out the pocket of my suit jacket that I'd neatly placed on my chair behind me. It was the burner phone I used when conducting my business with Kingston.

I glanced at the phone number that popped up before answering the device.

"You know you could have just called me on my regular phone."

"I wanted to keep business pertaining to you know what

off of our official lines. Hacking is a thing that could happen, you know."

He had a good point. "Well, get to it. What did you want to talk about?"

"We need to dig deeper here."

Those were the words I'd hoped he wouldn't say. That meant shifting my life more than I already had in order to maintain the secrecy around this sensitive issue because there was no way I could drag anyone else into this. I looked at the other phone on my desk and put it in my drawer.

I nodded my head although no one could see me. "Whatever you need from me, you got it."

5

MELISSA
PRESENT DAY

It hadn't taken long for me to prove my worth to Cross Industries. Damien and I worked together almost in lockstep. Whatever he needed assistance with at the office, I provided, on a strictly professional level. Although I'd have to be blind not to notice that my boss was attractive, I knew that I would be throwing my job away if anything were to occur. It wasn't something that I could afford to do.

"Melissa."

I snapped out of the light daydream I had been caught in, and I could feel a light blush come across my face. I'd apparently started daydreaming while I was eating lunch at my desk, and I quickly grabbed a napkin to wipe my lips before I answered.

"Yes, Mister—Damien?" It had taken a long time for me to stop calling him Mr. Cross. Although I still called Martin by his surname, it made it easier for everyone else if they were referred to by their first names.

"I have a meeting with Gage and my father in ten minutes. You're coming, right?" Damien dipped his head as he continued into his office, clearly assuming that I didn't have a conflict. Even if I did, I would have tried my best to cancel it.

"Yes," I said more confidently. "I'll be ready to go in a few minutes."

And that was true. Being on this job had taught me the value of being flexible because I didn't know what my workday would bring. When I first joined the company, I signed my weight in paperwork, detailing among many things how much debt I would incur if I said anything about what I knew as a result of my job. Given some of the things I'd seen over the years, I completely understood why those precautions were in place.

Damien strolled out of his office. "I'm going to head over to the main conference room on my father's floor to chat with him before the meeting."

I nodded and watched him leave. I still had a couple of minutes to eat lunch before I needed to head that way as well. Once I had taken a few more bites of my sandwich, I grabbed my laptop and my phone and left my desk.

Soon I stood several feet away from the heavy wooden door that would lead to one of the main conference rooms in Cross Industries. I assumed that Damien had already arrived since he left before I did. When I opened the door and slipped through, I saw that I wasn't the first person in the office.

Mr. Cross and Damien were already seated next to each other and Mr. Cross's secretary, Ellen, was across from them. I soon joined her and made myself look busy as I found an email to finish typing. I glanced at the time in the corner of my screen and noticed that it was after the start time that the calendar invitation had stated. Damien and Mr. Cross usually weren't late when it came to running meetings, and we all were here, so where was Gage Cross?

As if he'd heard me, the door opened and in strolled Gage. The look on his face told me that he wasn't even the least bit bothered about the fact that he was late. I expected to find Broderick behind him, but when Gage closed the door, I raised an eyebrow slightly before turning my attention back to my computer.

Mr. Cross cleared his throat. "Now that we are all here let's get started."

Gage smirked as he looked at his father. When he shifted his eyes and they landed on me, I unconsciously held my breath. For what reason? I couldn't quite explain.

I'd been in his presence before, but he usually didn't pay any attention to me. Now, his stare was focused on me, as if he was trying to discover every little detail. I let out the breath I was holding and turned my attention back to my boss, but that didn't seem to deter Gage. Out of the corner of my eye, I could see that he was solely focused on me, as if staring at me would solve all of the world's problems.

What has gotten into him?

"Broderick couldn't be with us today but had no problem with us continuing on without him."

"Interesting that the tables have flipped. The good twin has become the slacker, while the bad one is here and ready to have this meeting. I hope this is being noted."

Mr. Cross closed his eyes briefly before turning to his youngest son. "Gage, this is not the time nor place for this."

"I was just trying to lighten the mood a bit."

I glanced at Damien, who seemed to be used to their bickering, and Mr. Cross's secretary, who I was positive had a similar expression to the one that was on my face. We didn't sign up for these jobs to be in the presence of a family squabble.

Gage didn't seem to care about how awkward things had turned. In fact, the gleam in his eye told the room that he'd done it on purpose. Based on the brief interactions I'd had with him, I assumed he got off on doing things like that. I was willing to bet that he often got away with it too.

It was very easy to imagine that he got away with a lot of things. While he looked similar to his brothers, there was something about him that I couldn't pinpoint. It might explain the reasoning behind his desire to crack witty, cocky comments instead of answering seriously. What secrets he held, I'd probably never know, but I was intrigued. There was a darkness to his eyes that had nothing to do with his eye color. It reminded me of something, but I wasn't quite able to place it.

The Crosses continued the meeting, giving us updates on our current projects and answering our questions. Parts of it I felt could have been covered in an email, but I understood the desire to talk to each other face-to-face.

As the meeting was winding down, Mr. Cross pushed back from the conference table and said, "If anyone calls and asks for any of us and you suspect that something is wrong, contact one of us immediately."

That raised alarms in my mind. "What's going on? Is this something that we should be expecting to happen?"

I made it my mission to remain relatively quiet so as not to draw attention to myself. I'd gotten through most of my life by doing that so what caused this most recent outburst, I had no idea. After a few beats, it didn't take much for me to connect my feelings toward this to the reason why I left home.

I hadn't heard anything else in months, but that didn't mean that I didn't live on the edge of my seat, waiting for the moment that the world I worked so hard to build would come tumbling down.

"There's nothing you need to worry about. We'll take care of it."

I whipped my head around and narrowed my eyes at Gage. This was the first time I could ever remember directly talking to him during my time at Cross Industries and he decided to be condescending to me? Not a chance in hell. "I have the right to be worried about my safety. Don't talk down to me."

I regretted my last sentence, but only because I'd said it in front of my bosses. When I thought about this moment again in the comfort of my own apartment, I knew I'd blame it on me being on edge because of the email I'd received a few months ago. I could feel a blush creeping along my face and Gage confirmed it with a smirk on his face.

Mr. Cross cleared his throat. "We are taking precautions just in case, and a lot of this has been done before due to threats that have been made. A company email will be going out shortly, but we wanted you both to know since you work directly with the faces of Cross Industries and if anyone was going to be a potential target of such attacks, it might be you. Outside of our families, you are probably the quickest way to get our attention."

When Mr. Cross paused, Damien spoke up. "If you feel

that you need more protection outside of what is being provided here, let me know."

I raised an eyebrow and slowly nodded my head, not fully understanding what I was getting into. In the few years that I'd worked at Cross Industries, nothing of this magnitude had happened to require me to need extra security. Yes, I'd heard about the things that Anais, Damien's fiancée, had gone through, but this seemed bigger than that and that was a huge deal. Would Damien be willing to explain more about this later? I admit that I was kept on a need-to-know basis, but if any of this was going to threaten my life, I thought I had a right to know.

I glared at Gage due to his earlier comment. He'd shifted his attention from me to look at his father, but I still had a clear view of the expression on his face.

It left me even more confused than I was after Mr. Cross delivered the news.

"This meeting is over, but Melissa, if you would stay behind for a few minutes. Damien and I had something that we wanted to discuss with you."

I nodded as I watched Gage and Ellen leave the room and all eyes turned to me.

Damien spoke first. "First, I want to say that you've done an impeccable job of being my assistant since you were hired. You took on a lot early on and have shown not only that you could handle the workload that was expected of you, but you also had no problem taking on things that were out of the ordinary."

There were a number of times that I'd taken on tasks like helping to set up a fake engagement announcement for both him and Anais. I'd expected to deal with some strange things in this job, but that was one of the strangest. Another weird thing was him complimenting me on my job especially in front of his father. I knew I was doing a good job, given what was discussed during my performance reviews as well as the lack of critiques I received and the bonuses that I was given, but Damien usually kept his opinions on such matters close to the chest.

"Thank you. It means a lot coming from you." That was the truth.

Damien gave me a tight smile. "With that being said, I know this wasn't where you pictured yourself being long term. I remember that when you came in for an interview, you mentioned that you were not only excited about this job, but about the ability to grow."

I nodded, somewhat impressed that he was able to recall that from a conversation we'd had years ago. I glanced at Mr. Cross briefly and found him slightly nodding his head, agreeing with his eldest son.

"The last thing I wanted to do is stifle your growth, even if I selfishly want to keep you as my assistant forever."

I couldn't stop the small smile that appeared on my lips. Mr. Cross shifted in his seat, and I turned my attention to him when it became clear that he was about to speak.

"As we've continued to grow, new positions become available. There are a couple that should be opening within a few months and one of those might be a perfect fit for you."

His words made me swallow hard. "Really?"

Mr. Cross nodded. "As I said it might take a few months for things to get settled, but we acquired this company, I had you in mind to help with managing it once we brought it under the Cross Industries umbrella."

Managing? He is kidding, right? "I'm speechless."

"But this is something you would want to do?"

"Heck yes!" I exclaimed, barely stopping myself from yelling a curse word. Didn't want either one of them to snatch this opportunity from me because I couldn't control my mouth.

"Excellent. Damien or I will keep you in the loop as the opportunity develops and we'll inform you of next steps when we have them. Congratulations, Melissa."

"Thank you. Thank you both so much." Trying to maintain a facade of being cool and calm was thrown out of the window. I nearly jumped out of my seat to eagerly shake both of their hands, before I gathered my things and left the two men in the conference room. The leap I took into applying for a job with Cross Industries continued to pay off for me and remained the constant good thing in my life.

6

MELISSA

"Melissa?"

It was a few days after the meeting where I found out about the promotion. I looked up from the email I was reading over. It had something to do with organizing a conference meeting with several CEOs from out of the country, and I wasn't looking forward to helping with it, so the interruption was more than welcome. Damien was standing in the doorway of his office, holding a couple of folders in his hand. "Yes?"

"Can you deliver these to Gage? He should be expecting them."

"Sure." I stood up and collected the files. I wasn't looking forward to bringing them to Gage, but I knew it would be a quick trip, so it was best to get it over with.

I smoothed down the yellow dress I'd worn today and walked toward the hallway that would lead me to the elevators. There was no way I was walking down or up the stairs if I could help it with these shoes. I mentally chastised myself for not thinking to put my flats on that I kept near my desk, but it wasn't worth turning back now to make the switch.

Soon, I found myself on Gage's floor. It hit me that in all my years at Cross Industries, I could probably count on one hand how many times I'd ventured to his floor. Although there wasn't much aesthetically different from Damien's floor, the energy felt different. From what I'd known about Gage in my very limited interactions with him, he'd always been the jokester out of the three Cross men but given the interaction I'd had with him during the meeting, I felt anything but light and airy. That was the same vibe I was getting as I made my way toward Gabe's office.

I wasn't surprised to find that the desk in front of his office was empty. It wasn't a secret that Gage had let another assistant go and the position had remained empty ever since. It would have been so much easier to hand these files off to my counterpart instead of taking them to him.

I reached Gage's closed door and knocked.

"Door's open." I opened the door and found Gage Cross sitting behind a monstrous desk. Thoughts that he might be overcompensating for something filtered into my mind, but I didn't voice them. *Just hand the files over to him and leave.*

"Well, well. This is a wonderful surprise." The way he said it told me that there was a hidden meaning behind his words. He let his eyes roam over my body as if he were committing everything he saw to memory. I didn't say anything as I watched him, caught in a trance as he examined me.

I coughed lightly to draw his attention back up to my face and said, "I'm just here to deliver these files to you."

With a slight hesitation, I walked over to his desk and

stretched my hand out, trying to keep as much distance as possible. He looked down at the files before looking back at me, not making any movement to take them out of my hand. Feeling awkward, I brought my arm back down to a resting position. "If you don't need these anymore, I'll—"

"Oh, I need these files, but I'm not letting you walk out of here just yet."

"Excuse me?"

His tone took me off guard although I should have been prepared for it, given the way he acted toward me in front of his father and brother.

He leaned back in his chair and said, "I wanted to talk to you for a moment. Take a seat."

"I'd rather stand."

"Suit yourself."

In the back of my mind, I didn't want him to tell any of his family members anything that could be misconstrued as me not doing my job, jeopardizing the promotion that I knew was within my reach in just a few short months.

"My outburst during the meeting with my father, Ellen, and Damien was out of line."

"Uh. Thank you?" Was this his way of apologizing? I didn't appreciate his outburst, but I didn't expect him or anyone else to bring it up again.

"You've worked here for a number of years, right?"

I was taken aback by his question. Had he not noticed all the times we'd both been in the same room together? "Uh yes. I've been at Cross Industries for a while."

"Interesting. Have you had any other positions other than working for Damien?"

Where was this line of conversation going? "No. I joined right after I graduated from college."

Instead of saying more, he continued to study me, making me feel slightly uncomfortable under his stare. I was sure most of this was in any file that Cross Industries kept on me, so what was with all of the questions? Especially from someone he hadn't realized existed until a few days ago? I needed to get out of here.

"Is there anything else you need from me?"

Gage shook his head. "I have a few ideas, but that will be all for now."

"You have a few ideas?" My question had more bite than I intended, but it was out there now.

He shrugged and turned back to his computer, essentially dismissing me from his office.

The conversation hadn't been the worst thing in the world, but the way he stared at me left me unnerved. It was as if he knew something that he wasn't ready to share and that frightened me. What the hell was that all about?

Whatever the case, I hoped that was the last time I had to interact with Gage for a long time.

∼

THE BEER in my hand landed on my table with a loud bang, thankfully not shattering the glass. I'd been taking the time to unwind after work and wasn't expecting to be interrupted. I was startled slightly by my phone vibrating and falling off the table.

Unknown Number: *I want to see you.*

That was probably the creepiest thing someone had ever

said to me as an introduction to a conversation. I debated blocking the number, but it was as if the person could read my mind because they sent another message.

Unknown Number: *It's the man that gave you the quickest orgasm you've ever had. And I plan on doing it again. Soon, in fact.*

My heart leapt into my throat. How could I be having this reaction over someone I briefly met? Oh, because we had mind-blowing sex that I still thought about daily. Blocking the number would have been easier, but I couldn't resist the urge to send a message back.

Me: *Absolutely not. It's not a good idea.*

I typed the words out before I could second-guess myself. I wasn't surprised to see that within a minute of me sending the message, I received one in return.

Unknown Number: *Why not, sweetheart?*

I could hear him saying it again and it sent a shiver down my spine. I thought about what going another around would mean and shook my head.

There was no way I was about to do this. This guy hadn't contacted me in months, yet I was ready and willing to meet up with him and let him fuck me again?

What had I turned into?

What had he turned me into?

I chastised myself for even entertaining the idea. There was no way I was going to see him.

Unknown number: *Wear the mask and we'll remain anonymous.*

The mask? Well, that wouldn't be too bad, and it would keep the mystery about who he was alive... I didn't even know if I wanted to see him again. Should I?

Absolutely not.

There was no way I was venturing down this path after eight months of silence. After he didn't reach out immediately following our rendezvous, I'd tossed out any thoughts of ever speaking to him again, but it felt good to know that I was still on his mind. That night rocked his world as much as it had mine.

But there was no way I was crawling back for another one-night stand.

Me: *We agreed that what happened that night would stay there. Have a nice life.*

I blocked the number and placed my phone down with a decisive thud. It felt good to be in control of something especially when it felt like the world was spinning out of control.

Between talks of the promotion and the email I'd received from someone I thought I'd left firmly in the past, my nerves were fried. With a heavy heart, I stood up from my seat on the couch and walked into my bedroom. Before I could register what I was doing, I was kneeling in front of the box that had been so many different things to me.

It was the reason why I was here.

It was the reason why I was still afraid.

I sifted through some of the papers that I'd placed inside of it years ago and found what they'd been protecting.

A USB drive that was about as big as my hand was my insurance policy and maybe one of the reasons I was still alive.

However, I couldn't help but feel that it was only a matter of time before it all would catch up with me.

7
GAGE

"So, what is this meeting all about?" Broderick asked.

I leaned back in my office chair hoping that this call would be over as quickly as possible. There were things that I needed to do that this family gathering was preventing me from tending to.

"Damn if I know," Damien responded. "Maybe it's Kingston going to confess that the reason why he drops by my apartment building more often than not to make sure that everything is okay is because he's hoping to catch a glimpse of Ellie."

I snorted as Kingston was about to respond when Dad spoke up. "Can I make an announcement first?"

"Sure, Uncle Martin."

Dad cleared his throat. "We have a bit of a personnel change. Since Gage cannot keep an assistant for longer than five seconds nowadays, we are going to shift things a bit. Melissa will be Gage's new assistant while Isabelle will be Damien's. Let's see how that situation works out."

"Dad, if you run off Melissa due to this, I'll—"

Dad interrupted Damien. "I think she can handle this."

I tried to respond before Kingston cut me off. "I really have something important to discuss."

"Go on, Kingston. We can talk about the assistant switch later."

"We need to talk about the hit that was put out on Grace."

I was fuming from Dad steamrolling over me but was able to calm down enough to hear Kingston speak. "Malcolm lied; he didn't put the hit out on Grace. He knew who did though."

Broderick narrowed his eyes and asked, "Wait, what? How do you know this?"

"We got this video sent to us today. Confirmed its authenticity. Let me share my screen."

"Broderick, you think that you've won," Malcolm said before a sickly smile appeared on his face. I was reminded that he uttered the same words before I slit his throat. "But this is far from over.

"See, I'm not the one who put a hit out on your girlfriend, but you should be anxious about who did. Because they are still out there, watching your every move. And I'm not just talking about you. I'm talking about your entire family.

"You all fucked with the wrong person and now it's time to pay the price." The video ended abruptly after that.

"Remember that we thought that someone else had to be funding Vincent in his endeavor to get revenge on Dad and to hurt Damien?"

"Yes, of course."

"This lines up with what Malcolm just said. There's someone else pulling the puppet strings who we know nothing about."

Dad cleared his throat. "This means that from now on, everyone on this call shouldn't take their security measures for granted. Who knows when or how this person will strike next."

The call continued, but a lot of what was said blended together due to the anger I was feeling about being dismissed. When we hung up, I almost tossed my laptop to the side in anger. Yes, I was the youngest on the call and had issues with listening to authority when I was younger but being blindsided and disrespected was way too far. If Dad wanted to discuss this offline, that was one thing, but doing this in front of others was out of line and out of pocket. I made a vow to rectify this the next time I saw him.

∞

I KNOCKED on my father's door on Monday and opened the door before he could welcome me in.

"Gage, I expected to see you." He didn't look up from his computer as he kept typing.

"I'm sure you did. I assume I don't have to explain why I'm here."

"No. It's best if we don't insult each other's intelligence in that regard."

I narrowed my eyes at my father. I had every reason to be pissed at what he did, but I wanted to know his reasoning because the likelihood of Martin Cross acting without a plan was about the same as a snowball being able to survive in the depths of hell. I closed the door behind me and didn't bother sitting down.

"How dare you assign me an assistant without my permission? And then to half ass mention it on a call with everyone else on it?"

Dad looked at me before he replied, "I could have done a better job when it came to tell you, but I don't regret assigning Melissa to work for you. I only feel bad that she now will be taking on another job because Isabelle isn't able to help Damien. I have given all of you a lot of autonomy when it comes to working for Cross Industries, and I let you do your own businesses on the side, but it becomes my problem when a sector of this empire that we've built isn't doing as well as I know it can be."

Anger began to build within me. "Are you saying I'm running my part of the business into the ground?"

The expression on his face told me that he didn't think I was being serious. "No. My goal is to give you one of the tools that I believe you can use to succeed. You have so much potential, but it's seemed stagnant over the last few months, and I know whatever is going on in your life you don't want to talk about it with your brothers."

Of course, they'd been talking about what they suspected I was up to. That's what they'd been doing for most of my life especially when they thought I fucked something up. Yes, what I'd been doing outside of company hours had taken up a significant portion of my time, but I knew there was no way that they knew what was going on.

Every time they found out about the things that were going on in my life, they tried their best to get me to toe the line that they set out for me. It was better when I kept things private, away from them, but I wondered if this was Dad's way of trying to find out what I was up to.

"If you've given me autonomy over my businesses, then

you shouldn't have made Melissa my assistant. It's clear that your version of independence is bullshit."

The look Dad gave me reminded me of the expression that would switch on when he was pissed at us as kids. "I gave you plenty of opportunities to get your shit together and to keep an assistant for longer than two months. You need as much help as you can get, so I'm stepping in before things get worse. You've missed deadlines, have been late for meetings, and just a lack of organization and focus on your job here has been a problem for far too long and who knows why. It's time to put an end to this."

"I planned on hiring someone to help me on my own time."

"The hell you did. You're too busy with your extracurricular activities to get things done. Probably spending too much time at Elevate to do anything else."

He didn't know what the fuck he was talking about, but another thought came to mind. "You switched her responsibilities so that she could spy on me."

This was reminiscent of a time in my life that I tried to forget but couldn't. It drove my desire to get even.

Dad scoffed. "Absolutely not. She has no idea that this arrangement is occurring yet. And I know when you are ready to come forward with whatever is going on, you will. I trust you."

I could hear the sincerity in his words, but it didn't make me any happier about what was happening.

Dad continued, "She's just there to help you while you find another assistant. She's one of the best and will do a lot to help you move everything forward around here."

"Okay, but if it's not a good fit—"

"She'll go back to working for Damien full-time, but I think you'll find her more helpful than not."

"Whatever." I turned around to walk out of his office. This conversation was over.

"Son?"

Dad's voice stopped my progression, and I rested my hand on the doorknob, ready to put this conversation behind me. I didn't turn around to face him.

"I hope that whatever has troubled you off and on for the last few months gets better. And when you are ready to talk, I can speak for both your mother and me and tell you that we are ready to listen."

Instead of replying, I walked out of his office, slamming the door behind me.

8

MELISSA

"Melissa, can I speak to you for a moment?"

I was shocked to find Mr. Cross in front of me.

"Damien's not here, but he should be back—"

"I know he's not here and I came to talk to you. He was supposed to be back for this, but he got held up. He told me that he'd catch up with you later. Can we speak in his office?"

"Uh. Yeah. Sure." It felt weird entering Damien's office without him being there, but it felt just as weird talking to Mr. Cross alone. I'd talked to Mr. Cross alone only a handful of times outside of when he greeted me in passing around the office.

Once we both sat down at a small table in Damien's office, Mr. Cross said, "We are shifting your responsibilities around a bit earlier than planned."

His comment made me sit up a little straighter, but I could hear a large *but* that should have been at the end of his comment.

"What does that mean?"

"We want you to start working as Gage's assistant too."

"Wait what? Are you serious?"

"Very."

Any sense of professional decorum went out the window. "I thought I was doing a great job working for Damien and that I was on top of the list for one of the new management positions opening up soon?"

"You are. And that's why we believe that you can handle working for Gage. Of course, with this move comes an increase in salary and the potential for a higher bonus at the end of the year."

"Do I have time to think about this? It would be an adjustment for me."

"Of course you do. You're one of our star employees here at Cross Industries and I view this as a way to make things move much smoother across the divisions here. Once we have a more permanent plan in place or your new promotion is ready to go, we'll shift things around and you'll no longer be working with Gage."

Could no one else do this? Why did this feel like it was a test to see how well I'd be able to keep it together under this pressure?

"Would I still be working with Damien as well?"

Mr. Cross nodded. "You'll be working with Gage eighty percent of the time and Damien twenty percent of the time."

Working with Gage that much didn't sit well with me, but at least I would still have some parts of my last job.

"Does this make sense? Any questions?"

I shook my head. "No. I understand completely."

The one question I had was whether or not I would

survive this, but neither I nor Mr. Cross had the answer to that.

∽

"I SORT OF GOT A PROMOTION."

"What do you mean, 'sort of'? Isn't a promotion usually a yes or no thing?"

Nia had called me once I'd gotten home for work, and I took the time to explain to her what my new role was at Cross Industries without spilling the details about what was supposed to be waiting for me in terms of the future of my job. I didn't want to tell anyone about the opportunity without things being official yet.

"I'm now working for both Damien and Gage Cross."

"Whoa, isn't that a lot?"

"I assume it will be more than what I'm used to, but I'm not sure what it looks like yet."

"They couldn't just hire someone to help in that position?"

I rolled my eyes. "If you only knew the number of assistants that he has gone through since I joined the company, you would see that it isn't as easy as you think it would be."

"Do you know the reason why he goes through so many assistants? I'm sure some of them have talked to you about what he's like before they left?"

I thought about her question for a moment before I replied. "There have been rumors here and there about why no one stays in the job for too long, but I don't know for sure because I've barely worked with him."

Nia cleared her throat. "In my opinion, I would be flattered that they thought you could handle what seems to be a contentious job. On the other hand, what is it going to do for your work life balance? It seems as if the common denominator in his assistants not lasting all that long is him, so what is working with him going to be like for you?"

I didn't have an answer for that. Being his assistant would be a new journey and it seemed that it would be a different road from the one that I was used to with Damien. It took some time for me to figure out how best to work with Damien, but it all worked out in the end. With Gage, I didn't know what tornado I was about to step into because he seemed to not have much patience when it came to having his assistant get their feet wet in the new role. I knew I would have to come out swinging in order to make a good impression.

"I'll probably be able to tell you that in a couple weeks, but he is not going to force me to leave my job at Cross Industries."

"Good. We can meet up for drinks and talk about it. We also need to talk about the guy you met at Kiki's party."

The shifting of topics almost gave me whiplash. The only time I thought about the mask guy was late at night when I was all alone. There were moments during those late nights when I nearly unblocked him, but then my rational brain kicked in and I kept him safely locked behind that blocked number.

"I'm glad you told him to fuck off after he waited so long to text you, but you mentioned how good the sex was and—"

"We agreed that it would be a one-time thing, so I wasn't really expecting him to text, and then when he did, I realized it wasn't something that I wanted to go back to doing. It felt as if I was circling back around to where I shouldn't be and that it would lead to nothing more, so why waste my time?"

"I respect that. I'm going on a date with Joel next week."

"Is that the guy from the sexy party?"

"Yes."

"Wow, he reached out?" I knew they'd been talking after their rendezvous, but I didn't know it had led to anything more, such as going on a date.

"He did! He'd been traveling a lot, and with my schedule, it has been hard to lock down a time, but we finally found something that worked. I was shocked as you are because I thought things would die eventually, but it hasn't."

"That makes me so happy for you. At least your one-night stand is on a path to turning into something more."

"Let's not get ahead of ourselves. He has plenty of opportunities to screw this up and then we're back to the drawing board. I'll let you know how it goes."

"Sounds good. I've a few things I want to finish around my apartment, so I'll talk to you later."

"Bye."

Almost as soon as I ended the call with Nia my phone rang again. I immediately recognized the area code, but the number was a mystery. I figured it was a spam call due to my phone number using the same area code and sent the call to voicemail.

9
GAGE

I looked at Melissa's information in our personnel files, determined to learn as much as I could about her before she officially started working for me. There was something about her that I couldn't place, and it had been bugging me for quite some time. Now that I had a second to do some research, it was time to get to the bottom of it. Starting with the file of basic information that Cross Industries had on her wouldn't tell me nearly everything I wanted to know, but it would tell me something. A starting point if you will. As I scanned her file, I was shocked to find that there wasn't much there.

I knew that she was somewhat younger than me, eight years to be exact. But other than the basic information that told me she grew up in Ohio, got her degree at NYU, where she currently lived and her cell phone number, I was able to learn only that she'd had no prior experience in business before coming to Cross Industries.

Dad and Damien let her join our company without knowing more information about her? Strange because I knew for a fact that most employees were put through the ringer before receiving a provisional offer that was contingent on whether or not something was found out about them. Yet, she'd gotten through with none of those things being done. *Strange.*

Figuring that it would make sense for me to have her phone number, I typed it into my phone and noticed that it was already in there under another name.

The woman from Kiki's party. The one who distracted me from the mission I'd hoped to complete.

I'd forgotten I put her number into my phone after I decided to ditch the burner phone and realized that that was probably the reason something was bugging me about her. Even though we'd fucked in the darkness of Kiki's party, my body still recognized the woman who had wrecked me. The one who stopped thoughts of having sex with anyone else due to my knowing that none of them would live up to the sexual encounter I had with her. A slow smirk crossed my face as I realized what had happened. What were the chances? I didn't think that anyone could make this up if they tried.

Why hadn't I noticed her before?

Oh, because I didn't want to fuck with someone that worked for the company, but seeing as we'd already done the deed, what was stopping us from going back for more?

Visions of our time at the party appeared in my brain and I was growing hard at the memory. What I wouldn't do to have her again.

After the brief text conversation that we had before I got rid of that burner phone, I chalked the experience up to being a night of indulgence and nothing more. I'd told myself

I had more important things to do even though she was never far from my mind, even when I couldn't afford for her to take up any extra mental space. But it turned out that she'd been right under my nose this whole time.

There was so much wrong with this, outside of her now being my subordinate. She didn't know that I knew who she was nor that I learned so much about her body and was begging to learn more. Yet when had I ever not grabbed a situation that had fallen so neatly into my lap? We could find a workaround because there was no questioning the fact that we would have sex again, it was just a matter of when. This was the first time since my father forced her upon me that I felt happy with his decision.

A quick check of the time told me that I had spent more time on my computer than I had planned. I stood up and flicked the light switch off as I was leaving the room. I walked down the hallway and strolled into my bedroom. Instead of stopping at my bed I went to the master bathroom, deciding that a shower was needed. Once the temperature was to my liking, I took my clothes off and stepped into the stall. The warm water fell over me, cascading down my body before reaching the floor. I'd hoped the shower would take my mind off of Melissa and our encounter at Kiki's party, but it only increased my desire to have her again.

Something told me that if I came clean and told her what I knew, she would hate me and want nothing to do with me. Then again, me being her boss now also threw a wrench in things. But when had I ever let a small detail such as that get in my way?

I ran a hand down my abdomen before enclosing my hand around my cock. The sounds that she made as she tried to hold back her moans while I was fucking her played on repeat in my mind, and my dick let me know that it was ready for another round with her.

My hand moved up and down my cock twice before I noticed the cum that had gathered on the head. I wiped the liquid before resuming the jerking motion with a newfound incentive to find my release.

I leaned my head back and allowed the water to beat down on my skin as I furiously moved my hand up and down my length, trying to reach climax. Now that I knew it was Melissa under that mask and wig, my thoughts switched from running a hand through her dark curls to pulling on them, forcing her head to turn up to mine. I wanted to see her body unclothed, on my bed, and in the light so that I could get a perfect picture just before I sank into her. In my mind, I could see what she looked like when she reached her peak, and the thought drove me to completion.

A low roar left my throat as I came, and my heart pounded in my chest. My forehead landed on the cool tile in front of me as I tried to catch my breath. Although I'd been with a couple of other women since we'd been together, it didn't feel anywhere near as pleasurable. It wasn't anything like what I felt when I was with her that night, but it would have to do. For now.

10

MELISSA

Although I was still planning on helping Damien while I could, I'd been told that I would primarily be working on Gage's floor, which sucked. I cleared out only some of my things, bringing only what I needed to do the job, before taking the elevator to Gage's floor. Once I reached my new desk, I sighed when I saw that his door was closed. I picked this time on purpose. If I was going to shift my entire work life to take on this new challenge, I wanted to have at least something that I could control even if it was just choosing what time of day I would switch desks.

I had to keep reminding myself that this was a new challenge that I would easily conquer because I had higher goals and ambitions beyond this job. And Gage Cross wasn't going to stop me from accomplishing them.

"Getting set up already?"

I jumped slightly as the voice interrupted my train of thought. "I thought you had a phone call that wouldn't end for another half an hour?"

After all, that was why I'd come down here now. I figured he would still be on the phone while I organized myself.

"It ended early."

Of course it did. I closed my eyes for a moment to steady myself before stopping what I was doing completely and turning to him. "Is there anything I can do to help you prepare for your next meeting? I think it's with Pryce?"

A smile played on his lips as he folded his arms across his chest. "You already know my schedule?"

"Since it's now my job to know your calendar, yes I do. Unless something appeared on it since I left my desk upstairs."

Shit, I shouldn't have said that out loud. I needed to keep focused on the promotion that I was going to receive and not Gage riling me up.

"Good to know. Once you're done here, I want you to get me a cup of coffee. Black, and then join me on my next call."

I bit back the retort that was sitting on my tongue. Never in the time that I was working for Damien had he ordered me to go and get him a coffee.

Promotion. Keep thinking about the promotion.

"Sure," I said through gritted teeth. This was probably why he never had an assistant last long, but he wasn't going to run me off. "Is there anything else that you need?"

Gage shook his head. "Not that I can think of."

"Then I'll see you just before the call is about to begin."

He lingered in the doorway for a moment after I dismissed him, due to probably not having expected me to do that. Instead of responding, he left and soon I was alone again. I placed the things I was still holding down on the desk and with a heavy sigh, walked in the direction of where I assumed the break room was. As I was preparing the coffee for Gage, I decided to get one for myself while I was there. During the process, someone else joined me.

"I don't think I've seen you on the floor before."

I glanced over my shoulder and found a blonde woman walking over to the sink. She was carrying a mug and I assumed she was getting ready to rinse it out.

I looked at her, while waiting for the coffee to finish brewing. "Ah. I'm Melissa. I just started working on this floor."

"Renee. Nice to meet you. What's your new position?"

"I'm Gage's new assistant."

Her mouth opened into an O shape before she could catch herself.

When her mouth snapped shut, I chuckled. "I bet I can guess what that reaction was for."

"I'm sorry. I don't want to change your opinion of what it's like to work for him, especially if you have just started."

"You won't. What have you heard or seen?"

"This isn't a slight against him, just things I've noticed. Overall, he's a good boss, but I've never been his assistant, so I don't know what it's like to work for him almost exclusively. He can be very particular, so sometimes it's just best to keep your head down and give him what he wants."

I could see that based on what I'd observed, but it didn't explain why he went through assistants so quickly. I guessed that would be something I would be finding out in time.

"I should get this coffee to him. It was nice chatting with you."

"Likewise. I'm sure I'll see you around."

With that, I left the break room with two coffees in hand

and slightly more knowledge about my new boss in my back pocket.

When I reached my desk, instead of stopping, I kept walking into Gage's office. He was seated at his desk, and I placed a coffee cup on either side of his desk. Without waiting for a reply from him, I walked back out to my desk, gathered what I thought I might need for the meeting, and walked back inside of his office before closing the door behind me.

I could feel Gage's eyes on me as I got settled in the chair in front of his desk. When I looked up, laptop set up to go and coffee in hand, I found him staring at me.

"What? Is there anything I'm missing?"

"Not at all. Ready?"

I nodded and he reached over and dialed us into one of the conference phone lines.

The meeting was underway a few minutes later and nothing of note happened. In fact, it was a boring meeting and I found that my eyes kept darting over to the clock on my laptop as I hoped that this meeting would end earlier than planned.

"Is there anything else that needs to be discussed?" I could have jumped for joy when Gage asked that two minutes later.

Although Gage was talking to Pryce and some of his employees, his eyes were focused on me.

"Everything sounds good on our end."

Gage nodded, but his eyes never left me. "Okay, we'll talk again next week."

Before anyone on the other end of the line could reply,

Gage hung up. I stretched my fingers as they had grown somewhat tired due to the typing I'd been doing.

"Not bad."

"Huh?"

"The call wasn't bad." He leaned back in his chair; his stare still focused on me. He glanced over at the shared document he had open on his computer before looking back at me. "Also, your notes are good. I can see why Damien wanted to keep you all to himself since you arrived here. What impressions did you get from the call?"

I was so stunned by him thinking that Damien was keeping me to himself that I almost forgot to answer.

"I thought the call went well and that they seemed to be interested in a number of avenues that would be both beneficial to them and to Cross Industries. He seemed to be more willing to take part in some of the projects that you suggested than others."

Gage dipped his head once but didn't tell me if I was right or wrong. He glanced at his laptop before he said, "I'm taking off."

"What do you mean you're taking off?"

"I have somewhere to be, so I'm leaving."

What the hell? "But you have a meeting with—"

"Reschedule it." He said it as if it was the simplest thing in the world. He grabbed his coat which had been resting on the back of his chair and put it on.

"That isn't the only meeting you have today."

"Reschedule everything through the rest of today. I'm sure you can handle that."

And he left me staring behind him without another word.

11

GAGE

"Didn't think you'd show up so soon."

"I'm full of surprises today."

Kingston slightly laughed. When he didn't say or do anything else, I narrowed my eyes and walked behind the desk so that I was standing over his shoulder. He called me here and then had the audacity to give me shit because I was on time. It wasn't uncommon for me to arrive late, so it should be expected. After all, he'd known me my whole life.

Kingston looked back at me, his face not showing any emotion. Instead, he turned back around and looked at the computer screen in front of him.

"What was it that you needed me to come over and see so quickly?" I thought about turning it into a joke, but this was no laughing matter. "I was planning on stopping by tomorrow evening."

"This couldn't wait. I'll let you watch this and tell me what you think."

It took a second for the video to start, but when it did, I crossed my arms as I watched the events on the screen unfold. It didn't take long for me to piece together that it was footage from the car chase that involved Broderick and Grace not too long ago. "How'd you get this footage? Someone had a drone and was taping the whole thing?"

"As if they knew it would happen. This is something I will share with everyone, but I wanted you to see it first given what we're doing together."

I nodded in agreement. "But where did you get the video from? You never answered that." I looked at Kingston briefly before turning my attention back to the screen.

"You'd be surprised who has no problem selling things to the highest bidder."

"Would I be? Given what we are doing together?"

Kingston shrugged. "Found out that someone was shopping a video that contained the footage of when Shadow was killed. Thankfully you can't see exactly when Broderick kills him, but I also didn't want the video to get into the wrong hands."

"Who's to say the person who took the video didn't make copies? Or had copies made for insurance?"

Kingston's eyes darkened. "I can't control who he sent it to before we got to him, but he won't be sending it out to anyone else, if that's what you mean."

I took that to mean that the individual was dead. That was probably a blessing in disguise for all of us. "Did he say who told him to get the footage? I assume he originally was planning on taping Shadow murdering Grace instead of his own murder, which could barely be seen in the video."

"After roughing him up a bit, he finally spit it out and handed me that as proof."

Kingston pointed to a piece of paper that was on his desk and I swore.

It was a business card with Kiki Hastings' name upon it. There was a phone number and an email address to reach her at, but nothing else. It was a way to keep her business under wraps.

"This is a good thing, isn't it? After all, you've been looking into her for a while."

Kingston didn't know the real reason why I'd been tracking her. I'd mentioned that I wanted to keep an eye on her for business reasons and he'd taken me at my word. While he helped me where he could, I appreciated him allowing me to take the lead on it and in return, I helped him with some of the projects he was working on.

"It could be especially if we trust that he wasn't lying to you." My response had more bite than I intended.

Kingston dipped his head. "There is a chance of that, but it wouldn't hurt to find out the connection between the two, would it?"

∽

I SLAMMED my hand on my dining room table, not caring about the pain that shot up my arm on impact.

I'd been at her party mere months ago and never thought to focus on Kiki while I was there. It made the fact that I fucked a woman there while I could have been trying to gather intel on Kiki more problematic in my mind.

So what if it had been hot sex that had blown my mind for weeks afterward? Who cared if I knew who this stranger was? All that consumed me was making sure that I got her into my bed where she belonged.

All of that had now been thrown out the window now that I had to figure out how Kiki was connected to all of this. There was no way that I would allow some fucked-up shit to happen to my family if I could prevent it.

I walked into my office with a new determination to figure out just what the hell was going on. I sat down in front of my laptop and downloaded the file that Kingston had sent me before I left his office. Before I got started looking over the information, I opened my email and typed out a quick message to Melissa.

M<small>ELISSA</small>,

I need you to set up a meeting with Kiki Hastings. Her personal assistant's contact information should be in my files, which you have access to. Any time that we are both available will work for me and it needs to happen ASAP.

Gage

A<small>S</small> I <small>HIT SEND</small>, I realized that there was a good chance that Melissa also had some interaction with Kiki due to her being at the party. I smiled as I looked at the time. It was after work hours so chances were I wouldn't get a response to my message anyway.

I switched tabs and shifted my focus back to the documents in front of me. What I was able to gather from them was that Kiki, much like Malcolm, the guy who tried to fuck over Broderick and hired a hitman to kill Grace, was connected to a shit ton of people in this city. That news didn't shock me given what I remembered about her from my mom, and it made sense given the world that she operated in: high-class escorts. Well, at least that was what she was known for. I suspected she dabbled in other areas, which I was sure if I read through the entire file, I would be able to confirm.

12

MELISSA

I could kill Gage if I knew I wouldn't end up in jail over it. And there was no way that I would do well in jail.

I tapped the key that he gave me just before he left yesterday evening on the counter as I waited for the order I needed to pick up. Once again, Gage told me that I had to do another minuscule task for him: pick up his dry cleaning and deliver it to his apartment. I got the feeling that he wanted me to complain to Mr. Cross about how he was treating me, but I refused to give him that satisfaction. I was determined to come out of this on top and if that meant having to deal with his stupid antics, then so be it.

"Here you go, Miss."

"Thank you," I said, grabbed the garments, and adjusted the strap of my purse. I left the cleaners and walked the two blocks to Gage's house, feeling my rage increase further. Not only was Gage's apartment out of the way from the office, but it struck me as to how easy it would have been for him to do this versus me. I mumbled cuss words under my breath as I walked into his apartment building and stood there momentarily stunned. It was as if I was transported into another dimension once I walked through the front doors.

When I found Gage's home address, I knew that he lived in a wealthy part of town. What I hadn't envisioned was an apartment in one of the exclusive buildings in the city that went for millions of dollars. And it wasn't as if these apartments were your standard one-bedroom apartment. Some of them were larger than some homes and could be thousands of square feet.

"Can I help you?"

I turned to face the voice and gave a small smile. "Ah, yes. I'm here to drop off something for Gage Cross." I gestured to the clothes that were draped across my arm.

"He said we should expect you. Did he give you a key to his place?"

I nodded, suddenly feeling nervous about having a key to his place.

"Excellent. Just sign in here and take the elevator to the 25th floor."

I signed my signature and wrote today's date into the box next to it before thanking the employee sitting at the concierge desk and walking to the elevators. As the elevator ascended, the more nervous I grew. Once I walked off the elevator and stood in front of his apartment door, I froze. It felt weird being this close to his home.

With a deep breath, I knocked and waited to see if I heard anything. When I heard nothing, but silence, I used the key that he gave me to open the front door. What greeted me wasn't all that shocking. The décor that I could see from where I was, reminded me of some of the design choices that Damien made to fill his penthouse's space. What made Gage's space different was the messiness that sat on his kitchen countertop. It looked lived in versus the spotlessness I remembered from Damien's.

"Hello?" I asked and yet again, I heard nothing in response.

Don't snoop. I repeated that mantra over and over to myself even though the urge to do so was strong. I needed to lay these clothes over a chair and then go back to work because I'd wasted so much time coming out here to deliver them.

I walked over to his couch and laid the clothes over the back of it, in hopes that it would keep the suit and button-down shirt as wrinkle-free as possible. I pulled out my phone to send Gage a text message but before I could press send, I froze. I'd heard a noise coming from behind me and I wasn't sure how to react.

With my phone clutched in my hand, I turned around to face the front door and said, "Hello?"

Instead of getting a response back, Gage Cross walked into the room with just a towel around his waist. "I thought I heard a noise coming from in here."

I was momentarily stunned into silence because I couldn't believe that my boss had just walked into his living room without any clothes on. It was clear that he took very good care of his body and the slight sheen of water from what I assumed was a shower only highlighted that.

"You didn't hear me when I knocked on the door or said hello?"

"No, I was in the bathroom as you can clearly see."

When he gestured back to his chest, I couldn't help, but stare. It had been months since I had sex and just looking at him was getting to me. But my annoyance had taken over.

"So you were at home today."

He looked at me as if I was losing my mind. "I was."

"Which means you could have picked up your own clothes."

Instead of answering, I watched as a smile creeped along his face and I almost saw red. The urge to snap at him was strong and the only thing that saved us both was that I remembered that he was still, in the end, my temporary boss.

The filter that I kept on my mouth was long gone. "Do you get off on annoying me? Asking for future reference."

The smile on his face got wider as he adjusted the towel. When it started drifting lower, I bit the corner of my lip. Part of me hoped he would end up being stark naked in front of me, which would be a treat based on what he was clearly hiding under his suits. The other part of me realized how unfair it was that he had more money than I could probably ever dream of and the looks as well.

"No. I don't get off on annoying you. But watching that blush appear on your face is becoming an aphrodisiac for me. And I can't help but to find more ways to make you blush."

My eyes widened at his words. The tingling that I felt traveling through my body went into overdrive and before either of us could do something stupid, I tossed my phone into my purse and walked around him, making sure to keep a lot of distance between me and the man who'd decided that continuing to stand here in nothing but a towel was appropriate.

Without another word, I walked to the front door and just before I could close it behind me, his voice stopped me.

"Melissa?"

I looked over my shoulder at Gage, waiting for him to continue.

"See you around the office."

13

GAGE

I was an asshole, and I had no problem admitting it. There were moments when I tried my best to be nice, but I often failed, unless I was talking to my mother.

Melissa had been on the receiving end of that treatment after the Pryce call and had done her best to avoid me ever since. I'd had to get creative in finding ways to see her, such as picking up my dry cleaning. Seeing the look on her face when I'd come out in nothing, but a towel told me I was pissing her off.

I couldn't say I blamed her, but it made it slightly more difficult for us to work together when she was either angry or just plain avoiding me. That would change right now. I smirked as I typed up an email to Melissa that I knew was going to irritate her. It was 4:45 p.m. on a Friday evening and based on what I saw from her as I was walking back into my office, she was eager to get out of here. The bouncing of her foot as she read something on her computer monitor and her bag that was already packed gave her away.

Too bad she wouldn't be leaving anytime soon.

"You wanted to see me?"

I could have easily told her what I wanted her to do when I walked past her but sending her an email telling her I wanted to see her was more fun.

"Close the door and have a seat."

She did as told, and I couldn't deny that watching her do as I said was thrilling. I couldn't wait to order her around while I fucked her again too.

"I hope you don't have any plans tonight, because I need your help."

Her mouth opened, but no words came out. Was I an asshole for requiring her to stay later than normal on a Friday night? Yes. Was I using this as an excuse to get closer to her? Definitely.

This project could have waited until next week, but I knew it would get Dad off my back if I was working on it now. Being proactive and all that shit. But what drove me more was being able to spend time with her, giving me an opportunity to learn more about her.

"I need you to find out everything there is to know about Pryce."

"Isn't he coming here for that business meeting in a couple of months?"

I nodded without giving her more details. I watched as she processed what I said.

"Can I be frank?"

I wondered where this was going. "Sure."

"Why can't this wait 'til next week? Mr. Cross mentioned that he didn't expect any preparation for this meeting to start until then."

Although she made sure to keep her tone professional, I

could hear the bite at the end of her comment. "Did you question things that Damien told you to do?"

Based on how wide her eyes became, it was obvious that my question had been unexpected. Good.

"No."

"Same rules apply here. It's almost as if you are determined to not be near me right now."

I hid my smile when she stayed silent, and I knew I'd hit the bull's-eye.

"Set your stuff up on that table over here and every time you find something that you think is important about him, tell me."

Melissa finally spoke up again. "But I could just write up a report for you at the end—"

"That wasn't what I asked you to do, now was it?"

She slowly shook her head and stood up without saying another word. When I saw her unpacking her bag, I couldn't help but smile. This would be a fun evening.

~

"Do you want anything for dinner?"

It was 7:17 p.m. and Melissa and I were still in the office. She was busy telling me things that she'd found on Pryce and compiling a cheat sheet on him, while I was busy reading documents that had been attached to an email from Dad to my brothers and me. When I took a break, I noticed what time it was and that neither of us had eaten anything since lunch.

She jumped when I spoke, my words clearly startling her.

I could see her debating with herself about what she was going to say. "Sure."

"Do you have a preference? Any dietary restrictions?"

"How about pizza? I'm allergic to pineapple so not having any on it would be great. I'm good with any other toppings."

"I'm going to avoid walking into the debate about whether pineapple belongs on pizza. Are you sure that's what you want?"

I expected her to say something more expensive since this would be on Cross Industries' dime, but she nodded her head.

"Pizza sounds great. I'll order it and you continue working."

She did as she said she was going to do. But I didn't. Instead, I watched as she ordered our dinner and charged it to the company card. The silkiness of her voice forced me to recount anything that would force the hard-on that was growing for her down. That wouldn't get us anywhere productive unless it involved me stripping her bare and taking her on my desk.

Instead of making a move like I wanted to, I held back, knowing that right now wasn't the right moment. But it soon would come and when it did, Melissa wouldn't have a shred of armor to wrap herself in that would protect her from what I wanted to do.

Satisfied with that for now, I turned back to my computer, ready to continue working as we waited for our food to arrive. Thankfully it didn't take long, and I went downstairs to grab the pizza, while Melissa kept working on the Pryce project.

She looked up when I came back into the room and as I was placing the food on the table her phone rang, causing her to jump. Melissa looked down at the device and something came over her face just before she clicked it off. I watched her for a few seconds and noticed that she stared off into the distance as if no one else were in the room but her.

"Who was that?" I asked.

"No one."

I folded my arms over my chest. What was she hiding? "It sure didn't look like that wasn't anyone."

She slowly turned her head to look at me and I could feel the irritation through her glare. "Why do you care? It has nothing to do with you."

Her feistiness intrigued me, and her question was valid. Why did I care? Instead of answering her question I said, "If it takes away from your ability to do this project, then it is my problem."

"It's not. I'll get back to work right now." With that, she dug her head back down into her laptop, not bothering to touch the pizza that was lying in the box just several inches away.

Without any prompting, I grabbed a couple of slices and placed them on a plate before sliding it over to her. She looked up at me briefly before turning her attention back to the laptop, determined to prove that she was fine. Even when I knew she wasn't. There was so much that she thought she could hide from me, but what she didn't know was that I was already in the process of learning everything about her, breaking down her defenses every step of the way.

14

MELISSA

"I'll take you home."

His voice startled me out of the daydream I'd thrown myself back into. We'd finished eating a couple of hours ago and it had to be getting close to 10 p.m. Here I had spent way more time at the office than I'd planned, but it would all be worth it if I could get through this position as Gage's assistant. Or so I told myself over the last few hours.

At least the project had been interesting. With Damien, I had done my fair share of researching different people that he was either going to meet with or was thinking about meeting with, so having to dig through the information that Dave, one of the investigators that Cross Industries employed, wasn't a hardship. In my opinion, it made Cross Industries more resilient because they did their homework before making a move. I found it intriguing that this was a step that Gage wanted to take, given what I had seen of him over the last few days as we worked side by side.

He had a way of acting more on instinct versus gathering as much information as possible in order to make an informed decision. I could imagine that his different approach to the business drove his father and brothers crazy. So, what about Pryce had him pulling out all the stops before this big meeting that was supposed to happen in about a month?

I turned to him, finally ready to answer. "I can take the subway home, it's fine."

"No, I'll take you home."

Although I was staring at him hard, he refused to turn to look at me. It seemed as if his mind was completely made up and I would just go along with the program.

"Gage, I've been on my own for a long time now, and I've gone home after dark from Cross Industries before. I don't need you to take me home."

I felt silly even having to explain myself to him, yet I had. What the heck was that all about?

He finally turned to look at me, and his gaze sent a shiver down my spine. I hadn't paid as much attention to how dark his eyes were before, but they seemed almost pitch black and I was pretty sure they hadn't been that way before. The cockiness that he exhibited usually was still there, but there was a tinge of darkness that hadn't been there when we were diligently working over the course of the last few hours.

It was long after everyone had gone home from the office, yet when he took a step toward me, I still looked over to see if anyone was watching. Of course, there was no one there. I looked back over at Gage, he took another step toward me, and before I knew it, he closed the distance between us. Having him as close to me felt way more intimate, nothing like what it should feel like between a boss and his subordinate, yet neither one of us moved, even though we both had the ability to do so.

Although I knew that I should stop him from proceeding, the words died on my lips as I stared at him, wondering what he was about to do next.

He tucked a piece of my curly brown hair behind my ear before his hand caressed my cheek. The tenderness of his touch was in direct conflict with the look in his eye, telling me that the thoughts that were filtering through his mind were anything but sweet or innocent.

"Cross Industries is supposed to be on heightened alert, remember? What would I look like if I let you go home on the subway all alone? That wouldn't make me much of a gentleman, now would it?"

"You and the word *gentleman* do not belong in the same book together, let alone the same sentence."

His chuckle sent warmth through me, something I hadn't felt since the night of my one-night stand. I slightly adjusted my stance, hoping to hide the fact that I had to clamp my thighs together in order to remain standing. I wondered if he was going to kiss me, and deep down I hoped that he would. All rational thought about the power dynamic in our relationship had flown out the window and I was perfectly okay with that.

He leaned closer to me but instead of coming toward my lips he turned his head to my hair and whispered in my ear, "That's one of the few things you've gotten right while you've been in my presence, Miss St. Hill. It would best serve you to remember that. Now pack your things so we can go."

Disappointment surged through me when he took a step back. Based on the new look in his eyes, he knew what kind of effect he'd had on me. The smirk that appeared sealed the deal and I thought about slapping it off his face. An assault charge wouldn't look great on my performance review or when it came to getting a promotion.

Instead of arguing with him to further delay my getting home, I walked around him and packed my things. Given what time of night it was, traffic should be lighter, meaning that this trip wouldn't take nearly as long. The faster I got away from him, the better.

I packed up my things and walked to his office door where he was waiting for me. He didn't say a word before leaving the room and I followed behind him. The reprieve that I got from not having to talk to him due to his determination to get us to wherever he'd parked his car was wonderful.

It gave me time to calm down the jitters that I felt when I was in his presence. His insistence to drive me home raised alarm bells in my mind, but not the ones that I would've thought. My gut was telling me that he wasn't doing this out of the goodness of his heart. After all, after having worked for him for a week I was already able to deduce that a lot of the things he did were for his own benefit. Now it was a question of what he got out of this.

It didn't take long for us to get to the parking garage underneath Cross Industries. It made sense that he would park here because there was a lack of parking spaces near this building, and he had a specific spot that was kept for him. At this time of night, the garage was empty but during the middle of the day, it would be packed. And that wasn't including the number of employees who took public transportation to their jobs here.

Gage's car was easy to point out without looking for the

nameplate in front of it because of the lack of other cars in the garage. It was also likely the most expensive car that I'd probably ever been in the presence of. I couldn't figure out what the manufacturer was from where I was standing, but it looked expensive. It didn't surprise me that he'd bought the car in a bright red because the impression that I gathered from Gage was that he wanted to be seen at every possible opportunity.

I was surprised that he opened the passenger-side door for me. He barely showed manners outside of what you might find from a Neanderthal, so I thought he wouldn't do something as simple as opening or holding a door. Once I was inside and settled, he closed the door and walked around the front of the car. I followed him with my eyes, allowing myself to take all of him in. There was no denying how handsome he was even in the harsh light of the parking garage. It was almost unfair because I was sure that I looked like something that had gotten run over twice due to how many hours I'd spent at the office today without an opportunity to check my appearance in the mirror. Even his profile was a work of art.

The slope of his nose, down to the sharpness of his jaw, made me wish that he'd taken things further back in his office.

Melissa, pull yourself together.

There was no reason I should be thinking about my boss like that, even if my time as his assistant was temporary.

My fascination with him ended when he opened the driver-side door and folded his body into the car seat. The jitters returned because now I was alone with him for the period of time that it would take to get to my apartment.

The silence between us continued as he backed out of the parking space and drove through the garage. I kept my eyes straight ahead for the most part, with small glances out of the passenger-side window in an effort to not stare at him. I could feel my nervous energy flowing off of me in waves, whereas the energy coming off of him was pure confidence. He was secure in what he was doing at this very moment and around me. I chalked that up to him being in complete control and having power over me, at least when it came to work.

"Where am I dropping you off?"

I rattled off the address of the apartment that working at Cross Industries had given me the ability to afford. I leaned back in the seat and thought about closing my eyes when my head touched the headrest.

"Do you drive?"

His question took me by surprise. I expected him to break the silence first, but I hadn't expected that question. Small talk didn't seem to be his forte, yet here we were.

"Yes, I do, but I don't have a car in the city. It seems like it would be a pain to deal with, plus maintenance costs and all that."

"That makes sense. I probably wouldn't drive either if I didn't have a permanent parking spot at work. Sometimes I even take the train to work."

That caused my eyes to widen. "You do?"

He didn't turn to look at me. "What, just because I'm a member of the Cross Family, you think that means I don't take the train like everyone else does? How...presumptive of you."

"I wasn't being—" I stopped talking when I saw the small smile on his lips. He was fucking with me on purpose.

He chuckled when I shook my head. "Sometimes the train is more convenient so it would be silly not to use it. I only drove in today because I had something else to attend to before work."

I noted the slight change in his voice when he mentioned that he had something else to do before work, but I didn't ask about it. It was none of my business, and I didn't want to cross any lines.

The small talk continued, and I was both relieved and sad when he pulled up in front of my building. The ride had taken a little longer than I would have thought, and I wondered if he'd taken a long way to get to my home. Whatever, it didn't matter because I was home now.

"Thanks for the ride."

"No problem. You went above and beyond for me today by staying late and I hoped to return the favor."

I nodded, not sure what else to say in that instance, and moved to open my door. Except I was stopped by Gage's hand capturing my arm. There was pressure, but it was clear he wasn't trying to hurt me. Instead, he'd stopped me from leaving momentarily.

I looked down at the connection that we now had and just his touch made my pulse speed up tenfold. I looked into his eyes and was reminded of the look he'd given me in his office.

Lust.

Passion.

Danger.

The jitters that I thought had gone away during our

relaxing conversation as we rode to my home sped back up as I watched his head glide to mine. My eyes drifted closed without me processing what was happening and his lips landed on mine. The kiss remained light, as if he were testing the waters and not trying to dive into the deep end. Or so I thought.

When I felt one of his hands land on my cheek, the kiss evolved into something I couldn't describe. The magical moment felt familiar, yet not. What it had done was blow my mind and there was no way I should feel this type of way kissing my boss.

Wait a minute. I was kissing my boss.

As if he knew my dilemma, he broke the kiss first. When he pulled away, I took a couple of deep breaths that didn't feel like nearly enough. It was almost as if I was gasping for air, as if he almost stole my last breath.

"You know I can report what you did just now to HR."

"You won't."

He said it with all of the confidence in the world and he was right. I wouldn't because I wanted more.

15

GAGE

I was still thinking about that kiss days later and it was pissing me off.

I stupidly had hoped that kissing her the night I took her home would help get rid of the desire I had to have her once again, but it didn't. It only enhanced it, and it was just a kiss.

I'd spent the weekend thinking about it and was somewhat dreading coming into the office on Monday because of it. The pretty picture she'd painted as I watched her trying to catch her breath after that tumultuous kiss would be permanently etched in my mind. My thoughts wouldn't veer far from taking her on my desk and fucking her so thoroughly that her screams would tell the entire building just who was causing her to feel this much pleasure.

When I reached my floor, I turned my focus to work, no matter how hard it was to diverge from thoughts of her. What didn't go unnoticed by me however was that as I was approaching my office, she wasn't sitting at her desk like I thought she would be. Melissa was nowhere to be found, and while I debated trying to pinpoint where she might be, I decided instead to focus on work, which was my objective as soon as I stepped out of the elevator.

I didn't spare a glance at her desk as I walked into my office and sat down in my office chair. I turned on my computer and began reading through the emails that had come in either early this morning or over the weekend. After a few minutes of doing that, I heard some shuffling outside of my office door and looked up to see if it was Melissa outside. I was disappointed to find that it was just someone who was putting something on her desk.

Instead of trying to pretend that I was doing work, I pulled up her calendar to see if she put down the fact that she might be out of the office this morning. It turned out that she didn't list what she was doing, and I couldn't fight the desire to know what she was doing that required her to block off two hours in her calendar this morning.

Now wasn't the time to stalk my assistant, I checked my own calendar to see what calls and meetings I had today. When I found a meeting with Kiki that was to take place in an hour, I was surprised. I hadn't noticed the calendar notification over the weekend, but I was happy that Melissa had gotten the job done and that I would be meeting with this woman sooner rather than later.

What intrigued me was that the meeting would be taking place at her home versus in an office that I knew she kept in the city. That gave me the impression that she wanted to make this more personal than I had planned, but at least there might be fewer ears hanging around when I discussed the things I wanted to say.

I bent down and rifled one of the bigger drawers in my

desk and pulled out a burner phone. My fingers flew across the screen as I typed a message to Kingston.

Me: *I have a meeting set up with K.*

I hoped he didn't need me to spell out Kiki's name. Kingston replied almost immediately.

Kingston: *Good. That was quicker than we thought. I thought we learned that her calendar could be booked out for months.*

Me: *I know. Sounds like she really wants to meet with me? Then again, many people have broken meetings and events to be able to talk to us.*

It was no secret how much pull we had in the city, so it made sense that people would break their necks to score a meeting with us. Yet I couldn't stop the feeling that this wasn't the case with Kiki.

Kingston: *Do you have everything you need? I assume if you walked in there with a wire or any kind of device that could be used to record, she would find it.*

I had no doubts about that either. Given the security measures that we had to go through to get into her party, it seemed obvious that she might keep that security around to help her day-to-day, which raised my suspicions even more. What was she hiding or who was she hiding it from?

Me: *I think I have everything. If she is out to get me or any one of us, I assume she wouldn't pull the trigger during a one-on-one meeting. After all, it wouldn't be too hard to trace who I was meeting with given the fact that my assistant was the one who scheduled the meeting with her assistant.*

Hearing my father's warning again, for a moment I wondered if something might've happened to Melissa. I didn't trust Kiki as far as I could throw her, and it wouldn't be the first time that I'd heard about her using a form of retaliation to get her way. The other question I had was what exactly did she have to gain by doing all of this?

I stroked my chin for a second before I typed up an email to Melissa, asking her if she could send me the link to where she put the information that she gathered on Friday. I hoped due to her due diligence that she would reply relatively quickly if she could, letting me know without me having to come out and ask if she was okay.

While I waited, I typed another message to Kingston.

Me: *I'll let you know when I'm back and what happened.*

When I checked the time again, I noticed that I needed to get a move on if I was going to arrive at Kiki's place in time. As I was about to leave my desk, my computer pinged to let me know I just received an email.

It was a reply from Melissa containing the link to where the information was on our shared drive. Now that I knew that she was okay, I was fully focused on my meeting with Kiki. I did a couple of smaller tasks before I left my office to head to Kiki's home.

Kiki's place looked completely different from when I was last here. The main room where everyone had gathered to start having "fun" had been brightened up considerably and looked like your normal everyday entertaining room. The shift from night into day was a little startling, but not unheard of given some of the dealings that we all did. After all, Elevate could transform into your regular bar and restaurant relatively quickly if need be.

"Sir, may I take your coat?"

The woman who had opened the door for me was dressed conservatively in a black suit, but by the look in her eyes I knew that was where that ended. It was easy to see that she was undressing me with her eyes, and normally I might entertain going a round or two with her, but that thought was the furthest from my mind as I was preoccupied with a certain brunette who happened to work in my office and a meeting that was about to occur.

Although my brothers might say differently, I knew a lot of the actions that they took were a result of research and hard work. Of course, I'm not selling myself short, but my instincts played a large role in the moves that I made, and everything about this was telling me that something else was going on that I hadn't figured out yet.

"No, I'm just here to meet with Kiki."

"She should be down any moment, but if I can get you anything, and I mean anything —"

"Gage, I'm so happy you could come and meet with me."

I watched as Kiki walked downstairs, every step of hers displaying elegance that I was sure she wished she possessed. When she reached the bottom, she gave me a light hug without waiting to see if I reciprocated. Having her arms around me again after all of these years felt strange and I stiffened in response. When I pushed her away, something I hadn't done the last time we were alone together, she smiled. I'd almost bet she was reliving the moment just before Dad kicked her out of our home all those years ago. The gleam in her eye told me that was done on purpose to throw me off before we sat down and had our chat.

"Please follow me into my office. Do you want anything to drink or eat? I can have a member of my staff whip something up really quick."

"No, thank you."

When she glanced at me, I made sure to keep my face

passive to not give away anything that might be mistaken as a weakness to her.

Kiki brought me to a closed door and looked back at me before she opened it, leading me into a large room that was clearly her office. It was evident that there was no expense spared when it came to her office space, because she made sure that anyone who came to see her knew how wealthy she was. From the state-of-the-art computer on her desk to the gold-plated accessories that matched the theme throughout her house, she had no problem showing off.

She gestured for me to sit down in a chair. I was ready to be agreeable right now, on her turf, but if the tables turned, I had no problem getting nasty.

"So, what is it that brings you to me? Is there a woman you would like to entertain? I have plenty to choose from and I'm sure that I could find one that would fit your...tastes."

I didn't bother to shake my head because we both knew that she was full of shit. Instead, I decided to get right to the point of this "house call." "Why would someone who filmed a video that is of importance to me have your business card?"

"Can you be more specific about the video? And the person? I know a lot of people."

"Don't fuck with me, Kiki. You knew the reason I was setting up a meeting with you today had to do with that video."

She didn't answer, instead choosing to run a finger along the edge of her desk. It reminded me of when she ran a finger down my chest, aiming toward the boxers I'd been sleeping in. She was doing it to piss me off and to show that she was in control of the situation when in my mind she was anything but. The meeting might have been happening in her home, but there was so much dirt on her out there that I could make her life a living hell with a snap of my finger.

Kiki stopped her hand and looked up at me. "If the video you're referring to is about your dear twin brother and how he killed a man in cold blood, then yes I do know what you're talking about."

"Who wanted it to be filmed?"

"That I can't disclose."

"Like hell you can't."

The grin on her face turned wicked. "It's not like I didn't see you go upstairs with a lovely guest at my party. I think she was a friend of my personal shopper…"

I raised an eyebrow at her. "You do realize I'm the last person on Earth that you could hold something over on, right? Everyone knows I'm no saint and that there are skeletons that lie in my closet."

A knowing smile crossed her lips. "Are you sure about that? I would hazard a guess that there would be plenty of dirt about any of you to reveal to the public." She stood up from her chair and walked around to stand in front of me. "What about your cousin, Kingston? I'm sure he has some deep dark secrets of his own."

I clenched my fist. I had an idea of what she was getting at but kept my face blank. What did she know and how much?

"I'm not sure what you think you know, but I would tread carefully if I were you, Kiki."

"Or what? You're going to have me killed like your brother killed Malcolm? Bet you didn't think I knew that, did you? Or like he killed Shadow? Both of them were pussies and I've seen more than my fair share. I'm not afraid of anything you might think you have on me. Nothing has been able to stick, and it never will."

"That's because you've never come up against me before, and that's not counting the rest of my family."

She chuckled and I raised an eyebrow. I noticed a hint of nervousness in her laughter even though she portrayed herself as anything but.

I called her out on it and went with my gut. "You don't want to fuck around with us, but something else has you afraid. Deeper than anything that might be flung at you, including the legalities of several of the businesses that you run."

Shock registered on her face before anger. I'd struck a chord and I wasn't sure if she knew that I knew I had. There wasn't anything in the information that we'd gathered on her that indicated what I'd just said, but something told me to throw it out there and see if it stuck. It had.

"You warned me to tread lightly, Cross, but what you seem to not realize is that you should do the same. You and your family aren't the only big assholes in town, and it might be just about time for someone to knock you off the pedestal that you've placed yourselves on."

"Who are you afraid of? We can negotiate a deal where you're protected from any harm." Maybe trying a different approach would get her to reveal all.

Kiki scoffed. "By Cross Sentinel? Ha, they can't protect anyone, and it's foolish of you to offer even with you now working for them on the side. Now, leave my home."

16

MELISSA

It was clear that when Gage walked back into the office, he was angry. The slamming of the door was a huge indication. I assumed that whatever he needed to meet with Kiki about hadn't gone well, but it wasn't my place to ask.

I admit that when he asked me to set up a meeting with her, I almost threw up because I'd hoped to never hear or see her name again after the evening I'd spent at her home. Once I calmed down, I had no problems setting up the meeting, and I was sure that that would be one less thing that Gage could hold against me.

I was correct in that regard because I knew there was no way that he could be upset at me for doing what he told me to do. At least that stopped me from thinking about the kiss in his car and how that probably violated several rules that Cross Industries had put forth.

Although I tried to deny it, I liked it. I liked it a lot.

He was right that I had no plans of going to HR about it, but the kiss left a lot of things unresolved between us due to our job titles. It was a conversation that needed to happen, but it could wait if he was in a pissy mood.

"Melissa!"

The intrusion of his voice made me jump slightly. I hadn't heard him open his door and it took a moment for me to calm my racing heart. Since I didn't know what he wanted, I walked over to his door and looked in.

The furrowed brow that drew down into the cold look in his eyes was frightening, but still I stood firm. "Yes?"

"Close the door."

His words were tight, much like he looked to be as I closed the door.

"Lock it."

"Gage, I—"

"Lock it."

Without taking my eyes off of him, I locked the door and backed into it. Memories of that night at Kiki's floated back into my consciousness before I wiped them away as I examined the brooding man in front of me. That was when it happened.

I don't know how he was able to move so fast, but he was on me in a flash, kissing me as if it was the last thing he would do on Earth. This kiss was different from the one in the car. This one was more frantic, and I could feel his anger seeping off of him as he assaulted my lips. The urge to push him away was outweighed by the desire to pull him closer.

With that closeness came the discovery that his dick was making its presence known in a very big way. Lust tried to color my reasoning, but when I felt the bulge between us, I came to my senses. This had gone too far once again. My hands, which had been resting on his chest and had been grasping the hardness that was beneath my fingertips, pushed on him. He didn't resist and took a step back.

I spoke first. "You can't keep doing that."

"What's the problem? It would do us both a bit of good if you just admitted to how much you enjoy it when I kiss you like that."

"You already know why this is a problem. A big one and we didn't talk about you kissing me a few days ago."

It was fascinating to watch the cocky facade that he wore like a badge shift back into place. "I thought we were doing pretty good by not talking about it."

I recognized the diversion tactic just as he took a step toward me and ran his thumb across my lips. I was willing to bet he was taking joy in the state that he left my lips. Hell, in the state that he left me.

"We can't do this ever again."

"Why can't we? It's clear that we're very compatible. What occurred a few minutes ago proves it." He moved away from me and leaned against the corner of his desk with his arms crossed.

"I don't even like you."

It was a surprise it took this long for his smirk to appear. "Your body says differently."

This conversation needed to end now. "What happened in that meeting with Kiki that pissed you off?" I blurted the question out before I could stop myself.

His teasing smirk slowly left his face as if a switch had been flicked and he narrowed his eyes, his jaw clenching a little. "That isn't any of your concern."

I tried another approach. "How well do you know Kiki?"

"We move in the same circles. Why? And how are you on

a first-name basis with her?" His tone sounded accusatory, as if I'd done something wrong.

Although he hadn't moved, it felt as if his body was crowding me, imprisoning me without him having to lift a finger.

"I'm not. I just know I set up the meeting between you two and then you came back pissed. Of course, I don't know if you came in with a stick up your ass…" I bit my lip as the last part of my sentence came out. When he didn't look offended or about to fire me, I mentally thanked anyone I could think of that I still had a job. Then again, would he fire me if he had a problem keeping his hands and mouth off of me?

My eyes shot to his office phone when it rang, startling me out of my thoughts.

Gage didn't move at first, but he did when the phone rang a second time. "I shouldn't have lashed out at you over something that wasn't in your control."

He didn't look sorry. Not one bit. Nor did it answer the million and a half questions that were screaming at me in my head.

I used his incoming phone call as an excuse to leave his office. I quickly unlocked the door and scurried out as if my ass was on fire. I sat back down at my desk, wondering just how long I needed to stay here before I could leave work for the day.

A quick glance at my computer clock told me that I still had hours to go. *Shit.*

How was I going to make it through work and deal with all of this? My hands flew to my face as I tried to get myself together so that I could continue with the workday. Any composure that I might have had was on the floor where I'd left my dignity the moment Gage's lips met mine. I wanted to forget what had occurred in there, but I'd be lying to myself if I thought there was any chance I would.

"Melissa?"

I removed my hands from my face and looked at who spoke my name. It was Renee, who I met on my first day as Gage's assistant.

"Yes? How can I help you?"

"Would you be able to schedule time for my team to meet with Gage? Sometime next week would be preferred if he is available."

With a small nod, I turned to my laptop and pulled up Gage's schedule for next week. "Ah, it looks like he's going to be out of town at the beginning of the week, but I can get you on his calendar for next Thursday?"

She smiled at me. "That would be perfect. I'll send you the emails to send the calendar notification from you. I would have shot you an email, but I was walking past your desk and figured I could just stop by."

"Not a problem. Send me all of the corresponding information and I'll send out the calendar invite. If schedules change, let me know and I'll see what I can do."

"Perfect. Is everything okay with you?"

"Ah, yes. Just tired. I never get enough sleep."

"I understand that feeling. Well, I'll let you get back to work."

Just before Renee walked away, she gave me another smile. At least there was one person who was in a good mood today.

∼

"No, he didn't."

I rolled my eyes. "Nia, could you keep your voice down? I don't want everyone in this bar knowing all of my business."

She nodded and took a sip of her drink. We'd finally gotten together for an evening out and were catching each other up on our lives. She mentioned how the date went with the guy she met at Kiki's party and how they were scheduled to go out again soon, and I'd just filled her in on how I made out with my boss.

"It's clear that whatever Gage wants, he'll stop at nothing to get. What if that means you?"

"Nia, he's my boss."

"He's your *temporary* boss. And he's an attractive man that wants to jump your bones. What's so bad about that?"

"Oh, I don't know. The fact that he's my boss."

This time, she rolled her eyes. "Did you kiss him back?"

"Uh—"

She put her hand up. "And that was all that I needed to know."

"It's such a bad idea. Having sex with someone you work with."

"People do it all the time. You wouldn't be the first nor the last." She twisted the straw in her drink before she continued. "Look, I'm not pressuring you to do something you don't want to do—"

I let out a dry laugh before I glanced around to make sure that no one was trying to listen to our conversation. "You mean just like you didn't pressure me into going to Kiki's party?"

"I didn't pressure you into anything you didn't want to do.

I would have taken no for an answer if you weren't curious about what might happen that night."

She had me there, just like she had me when she asked if I'd kissed him back.

"Look, Mel, if what you're doing doesn't go against any of the rules, why not explore and see what happens? If that's what you want. If not, tell me to kick rocks."

I didn't tell her to do anything, because I was conflicted about what I wanted myself. Another swig of my beer was my answer instead.

"How did the rest of the week go?"

I shrugged. "It was quiet. Gage has a trip out of town soon and was starting to prepare for that. When he wasn't doing that, he was out of the office for one reason or another. Sometimes his calendar was blocked off, but other times he was just gone. I didn't ask any questions and sent him emails if anyone had any questions for him. It was nice to not have to be stressed about seeing him as much."

"And you two still haven't talked about either incident."

"Nope." I put the bottle up to my lips, letting the cool liquid flow down my throat. "I might just act like it never happened."

Nia snorted. "You might act that way, but I'm betting he won't once he gets back. It's clear that he wants you and I would hazard a guess and say that you want him too, given your non-answer."

"Can we talk about something else? Literally anything else?"

Nia chuckled and changed topics, which I was grateful for. However, she'd given me a lot to think about. The rest of our time together and my trip home was uneventful as I listened to all of the people around me who were also trying to make it home as soon as possible.

As I was walking from the subway to my home, my phone rang. Seeing the area code of yet another number I had to block, I quickly did so but before I could put my phone away, it rang again. When I proceeded to do the same thing, another number called me. Without thinking about it, I answered this time.

"What?" My question came out as a low growl.

The person on the other end didn't say anything and didn't stop me from talking.

"Stop calling this number."

There was a light buzzing noise on the other end of the line before the person finally spoke. "You better be ready, because I'm coming for what's mine."

I thought back to the USB that I was currently hiding in my closet. How had he gotten this number? I changed the same year I started college. Was he really going to make his way to New York City for it? And why now?

17
GAGE

I took the opportunity to look around Kingston's office. The space was sparsely decorated, much like the rest of his apartment. It was as if he came here only to rest his head and didn't take the time to decorate. Given what he'd been through, I understood his reasoning.

"So you know we've been keeping an eye on Kiki."

"Yes. You mentioned it in passing. It seemed like a good idea after the meeting we had. Have we found anything yet?"

Kingston shook his head. "Nothing that explicitly points to one of her conquests being who we are looking for. The biggest issue that we were having goes beyond just tracking her. We don't know how deep her connections go. Malcolm was relatively easy to track because more people talked on the inside about the deal that he was making, with whom, for what etc. This is different. Folks are keeping things about Kiki, the people that work for her, and who her clients are close to the chest. It doesn't help that she's mostly tight-lipped about it all as well. We're still digging, of course, but between NDAs and people wanting their transgressions to be kept hidden it's taking a lot more time."

Frustration bubbled under the surface as I had hoped for better news. There had to be some way to find out who Kiki's clients were. There was no way that she wouldn't have a list somewhere that she more than likely always had on her. Much like the guy who took the video of Broderick's killing of Shadow, it would be her insurance policy to keep her alive. Too bad it didn't end up helping him. I knew she dealt with some dangerous people, so there's no way that she didn't have some sort of way to track the people she was doing business with. From what I knew of her, Kiki was a smart, cunning woman. I would even go as far as to say that she could use that information as blackmail.

I leaned back in my chair and continued to think. Someone had to have something over her that was enough for her to employ another person to take what went down in Brentson. They were using her as a tool to not be found out. Why?

There was clearly something that was missing from the puzzle, and once we found it everything would become more clear. That was the thought that popped into my head.

"Is there a connection between Malcolm and Kiki? Since she had to know where Shadow was going to be, either she was told, or she had someone tracking Grace or Shadow or both of them in order to send someone to record what happened."

Kingston tapped his pen on his desk. "We dug into both of their backgrounds and couldn't find anything, but that doesn't mean that there isn't something there. We should also pull in Vincent. What was he up to in the years before he decided to go after Damien for something he deemed was the sins of Uncle Martin?"

I watched as Kingston stood up and shifted some of his things around so that we could see it. He'd already had Kiki and Malcolm listed, but quickly wrote down Vincent's name on a piece of paper before adding it to the board.

"Could Vincent and Malcolm have worked together? Coordinating a deal between the Vitale family and someone? It wasn't as if Vincent was completely estranged from the family for all of these years."

"That's a good theory. It would force us to question Will again and probably means we need to call Damien too."

Outside of all three parties doing devious shit to my family, I couldn't think of anything off the top of my head that would connect them. But there had to be something, and I was determined to find out.

~

As I drove away from Kingston's place, my phone rang, and I wasn't surprised to find that it was Broderick on the other line. I'd been so caught up in everything that I hadn't been keeping in touch as much as I usually did.

"Hey, man."

"Hi, I was wondering if you had time to talk."

My twin and I kept in contact regularly, but he usually didn't call just to chat. "Sure. I'm in the car right now, but that shouldn't be a problem."

"I wanted to circle back with you about whether or not you were going to be able to make it to Elevate's anniversary party? I sent you a text a couple of days ago, but never heard back."

Damn it. How had I missed that? "What date is the celebration again?"

"You don't know when we opened Elevate? What is going on with you? Are you back to doing whatever you refused to really talk to me about before again?"

A hint of guilt clouded my judgment. "Something like that. Why don't you and Damien meet me at my office tomorrow? I'll explain everything there."

It was about time I came clean. I hadn't wanted to burden the rest of my family with everything I was doing because they already had enough things to worry about including their significant others now. Plus, if we needed information about Will, Damien would be the best source before we did any more deep diving.

"About time." Although Broderick mumbled it under his breath, I heard him loud and clear. The next thing he said, he made sure I could hear. "The event at Elevate is in two weeks. Can you make it?"

"Believe so."

"Should I have them put you down for a plus-one?"

Here was another question I would have a hard time answering. An image of Melissa appeared in my mind before I answered. "Yeah, put me down with a plus-one. If I don't have anyone to go with, I'm sure I can find someone there to have fun with."

"Now that sounds like my baby brother."

"You're only two minutes older."

"Still counts."

I glanced at the phone before I responded. "Does it, Ric?"

A low growl came from the phone before I heard the call disconnect. Another point for me and none for Broderick.

I continued my drive and somehow, someway, I'd made it to Melissa's house without fully realizing it. I vaguely remembered typing it into my GPS, but between my need to leave Kingston's and my conversation with Broderick, I must have been super focused on getting out of there.

I ended up exactly where I wanted to be.

It was criminally obvious how easy it was to get into her apartment building, and when I knocked on her door, it was then that I wondered if she might still be awake. When I heard several locks click, I debated taking a small step back to give her some room. In the end I didn't, because it meant that I would be farther away from her, even if it was just a step.

"What are you doing here?"

"You. I came to see you."

18

MELISSA

My eyebrows rose as Gage shoved his way into my apartment. In almost no time, his mouth was on me. My mind was scrambled by the intrusion, but I did nothing to stop it because it was then and there that I was finally ready to admit that I wanted this too.

His touch drove me wild with anticipation as I wondered what his next move would be. As if he were reading my mind, I felt a slight tug on my hair, drawing my chin and lips upward.

"Are you going to tell me no?" His voice was raspy and raw, sending more tingles through my body.

The question wasn't much of one because there was no way, no how I was going to say no to the man in front of me. Throwing caution to the wind, I stood up on my tippy toes so that he would take my lips again, giving him the answer that we both craved.

He backed me into my couch, and I stared back up at him, waiting with bated breath.

"You don't realize how beautiful you look right now. Wide-eyed, mouth slightly open, aroused."

I was all of those things and wanted his hands back on me. Yet, I was stuck watching him undress and it was then that I realized what he was wearing. He'd come to my house in a black t-shirt and sweatpants, and all I could think of was how that meant easy access to his cock.

Sitting up, I reached for him, my hand landing on the waistband of his sweatpants. He arched a brow down at me and that trademark smirk of his spread across his lips. "I knew you couldn't keep your hands off of me."

I just shook my head at him and let my fingers trail over the waistband, before sliding them lower on his hips. The tip of his cock peeked out and I moved forward, licking it as my eyes went up to his face. He drew in a sharp breath as his hands went to the back of my head. Not forcefully, but almost, like he really wanted to direct me, but was waiting for some sign that I was willing.

I slid his pants down a little at a time, my tongue trailing down his cock as each bit of him was revealed to me. Finally, I took him into my mouth, sucking on him and watched him take a shuddering breath as his hands encouraged me to suck him harder.

After a few minutes, he tugged on my hair, drawing me off him. "Keep that up, Sweetheart, and I'm going to finish before we even start." He drew me up, his lips landing on mine, his tongue slipping between my parted lips, caressing my tongue.

Something about the way he said 'sweetheart' made my ears perk up, but he distracted me. His fingers left my hair, moving to my shirt, which he tugged up and over my head, tossing it aside. A moment later, my bra followed, and then my jeans and panties were being tugged over my hips and he was lifting me in his arms. I wrapped my legs around his waist and continued to kiss him.

I felt like a teenager all over again, high passion and hormones driving me to do things I normally wouldn't. Like fucking my boss. I was so screwed but at the moment, I didn't care. I could feel the tip of his cock at my entrance, and I wanted to impale myself on him, but he held my hips firmly, not letting me slide down on him. "Fuck me, Gage," I said through heated kisses.

"Bedroom?" he answered, his kisses moving to my jaw and then my neck, his voice husky with need.

"Down the hall," I answered, "second door." I moaned as his mouth landed on my nipple.

He moved us down the hallway and when he reached my room, he tossed me on the bed and then climbed on after me, moving up my body like a tiger stalking its prey. There was a light in his eyes that told me he was enjoying this. I reached for him, pulling his lips to mine and our kisses grew more heated. He moved off of me a moment later, his gaze connecting with mine as he kicked off his shoes and pulled a condom from his sweatpants pocket. Then he stood naked before me as he slid the condom over his cock and he moved back to the bed, settling back over me.

"I've been looking forward to this for months, sweetheart," he murmured. "Imagining you like this. Mine." He dipped his head down and kissed me again, and his cock slid home between my legs.

There was something familiar about the way he'd said that, but I had no time to think as he thrust into me urgently. I wrapped my arms around him as his mouth found my breasts again, kissing them, squeezing them in his hands. I arched my back, meeting his thrusts, panting at the pleasure of it and then I crossed the edge, screaming his name, "Gage!"

A few more thrusts and he too came, and his groan made me smile. I was sedated from the time we shared together and would worry about all that would come of this tomorrow.

19

GAGE

"Come in," I said without looking toward the door. I figured it was my brothers since Broderick told me that they would be coming down around this time. I just needed to wrap up one thing before I could meet with them.

I was reviewing a presentation that Melissa had put together and was incredibly impressed by the amount of effort she'd put into it. It didn't go unnoticed by me that she'd placed her own little anecdotes in some of the slides, and they made sense given the context.

Melissa finished her sentence before politely smiling as they entered. I stood up and clapped in response to what I'd just seen. "This is fantastic." I turned to my brothers and said, "I'm going to send you both a copy of this presentation because I know you'll be blown away just like I was."

I looked over at Melissa to see how she had taken my compliment and saw that her eyes had dropped to her shoes before it seemed like she realized what she'd done and forced herself to stand up tall. It took a lot to get a compliment out of me and she'd earned it.

"In fact, I was just going to see if you can get everything ready to go so that you could join me on this trip? I think it would be a great learning experience for you and you can help me with the presentation."

"Are you serious?" My words shocked her and the first expression that crossed her face was confusion, then anger, before she masked her emotions completely.

"Very. I want you to come with me and help represent Cross Industries to thousands of the world's business leaders."

I glanced at my brothers and saw Damien smiling at Melissa while Broderick was looking at me with an eyebrow raised. I ignored him.

She cleared her throat before she said, "I'd love to go. I'll get everything squared away."

The words she said didn't match the tone in her voice. It was clear that she was upset about something, but I wasn't sure what. I'd find out about that later.

There was no denying that what she'd done since she'd become my assistant was remarkable and I thought she deserved this opportunity. But I had nefarious reasons for wanting her there as well.

Three days of having her with me outside of the hectic world that we both moved in would be good for us both. It didn't hurt that the conference was taking place at some fancy resort in Hawaii, which would be a stunning backdrop to all of the ways I would be fucking her. No, those thoughts I planned to keep to myself, at least for now.

"Thanks again," Melissa said as she excused herself from the room and closed the door behind her.

"What a great thing for you to do for her," Damien said as he made himself comfortable in one of the chairs that I kept in my office.

"It's not something I'm doing for her. She earned it as I'm sure you noticed while she was working for you full-time."

Damien nodded. "Not to mention that she is now taking on more responsibilities for you but is still working on a few things for me."

"Shit, I should have asked you before I made that announcement to her."

Damien held his hand up. "I can get by without her for a couple of days. She should be able to enjoy this opportunity, and it might even help her as she transitions to her new role in the future."

I hadn't thought about the fact that this was a temporary situation in a while. Melissa had become so ingrained in my work life and made things so simple for me to manage that I'd gotten used to having her around and not having to worry that something wasn't getting done or that I would have to redo something that she did.

"I'd love to take a look at the slides. Dad said that she was up for a promotion, right?"

Broderick's question hung in the air for a moment before I responded. "Yes. I don't know when everything is supposed to be finalized, but that's the plan."

"Interesting. Even without looking at the slides, I do think she has helped you with your work here. I don't have to poke you twenty times to answer something outside of getting you to come to a party celebrating our nightclub."

If Broderick thought that he was going to rile me up, he was sadly mistaken. I was riding on a high due to my quick thinking. Getting Melissa to come with me on this trip was one of the most genius things I'd ever thought of.

"I already said I thought I was going so leave it at that. Or does it frustrate you that you're no longer the more productive twin?"

Broderick's head jerked back in response. "No. I just find it interesting that my brother, who is known for never missing a party, didn't respond to an invitation I was having at a spot that he co-owns. It's almost as if something else has your mind in a twist. The cockiness that you usually hide behind has dulled a bit too."

His comment stung. "Is this the path you really want to take?" I asked, looking forward to seeing what his response would be.

"Can you both cut it out? Neither one of you are kids anymore and I want to know why this meeting was called before we waste any more time. Okay?"

My twin and I nodded, but I couldn't pinpoint why Broderick's accusatory tone and questioning made me so on edge. I knew I was doing a heck of a lot better balancing my regular job and the things I was doing for Kingston on the side. I leaned into the jokester/partier persona that I had cultivated over the years to hide what I had been doing, yet him pushing that narrative on me right now was irritating. Maybe it would become less irritating once I got all this information off my chest.

"I asked you both to come down here to discuss the security issues we've been having over the last few months. I'm specifically talking about what happened with Anais and

Grace, and the warning that Kingston gave all of us during a joint call we had."

Broderick spoke up first. "And this has to do with the secrecy you've been displaying over the last few months?"

I nodded. "Yes, in a way. They're all connected in some fashion."

Broderick sat down in a chair next to Damien. "Well by all means, please proceed."

I, too, sat down in my office chair and before beginning, I used the remote that was on my desk to turn off the television that Melissa and I used to display her presentation. I then leaned back in my chair wondering how I should start the conversation and buy myself a few more seconds before I had to come clean.

With a deep breath I said, "For the past several months I've been working with Kingston. At first it was a way to use some of my expertise in moving through some of the professional circles that he or his employees might not have access to. Then gears shifted when it was clear that someone or some people were trying to harm our family. Starting with Anais."

Damien smiled for a second at my mention of Anais being family before he folded his hands and rested his chin on them. "So what you're telling me is that you're essentially living a double life in an effort to keep us all safe?"

I was living a double life in more ways than one, but I didn't need to divulge that. "Yes. We've been doing our best to keep you apprised of what was going on, but I've been helping Kingston more than we were both letting on."

"I'm impressed." I turned to look at Broderick as he continued. "I didn't know what to expect when you said you wanted to call this meeting, but to hear that you've been working with Kingston is a relief. While I assume that this is also dangerous, much like some of the things that we get involved in, I think we were all thinking what you were doing was so much worse."

I saw a flash of worry in his eyes, much different from the attitude he'd shown just moments before.

"I know and it made sense to try to keep things as quiet as possible. I didn't want either one of you trying to talk me out of it."

If this were any other situation, the looks on Damien's and Broderick's faces were comical, and I would've laughed.

Damien spoke first. "What do you mean? Why would we have to talk you out of doing something that you clearly wanted to do?"

"Because you two, and Dad for that matter, think that I'm not capable of doing some things or that I will probably screw it up in the long run. It's also why I've been given a small portion of Cross Industries. That way, in your eyes, there is no way I could fuck it up."

Damien and Broderick shared a look before turning back to me. "That's not—"

"Broderick, you don't have to deny it. It is clear as day to anyone who is paying attention. I've come to terms with it, and I decided to forge my own path, which has resulted in me helping Cross Sentinel."

"You know that Broderick and I had no say in how things were divided among the three of us."

"I know that. Dad set the example and you followed it. I'm not blaming either of you because it helped me to discover some of the things that I want to do in the long run that aren't directly connected to the Cross Industries brand. This is not saying I'm giving up my portion, this just helped me realize that there are other things that I want to do. And right now, the most important thing is that we need to find out who is trying to take down Cross Industries."

I changed the subject on purpose, not wanting to devolve into who thought this and who thought that. We had more important things to worry about.

Broderick ran a hand across his face. "Okay, so our key players as of now are Vincent and Malcolm. Vincent tried to do everything in his power to hurt Anais and Damien with the help of Carter. Then you have Malcolm, who hired a hitman to take out my girlfriend, not only because she was my girlfriend but because he suspected she might've overheard something while she was trying to rescue two men that weren't supposed to be saved."

I nodded. "And I can take over the story from here. We have someone who videotaped the Brentson incident between you and Shadow and was selling it to the highest bidder. Luckily Kingston's team got in and was able to get the video just before this person was killed. Turns out they found a business card and a note to Kiki Hastings."

Damien's hands dropped. "So he's connected to her in some way. I guess that's not unbelievable. Her connections run long and deep in the city."

"And that's the point. I met with her to try to find out if she was the one that was behind all of this, and if she wasn't then who told her to hire someone to tape the scene. Based on what she said, and her demeanor, whoever this key player is, is holding something heavy over her and she's much more afraid of that person than she is of what hell storm we could bring."

The room remained silent as my words hung in the air. It was a lot of information, so I understood the moment needed to process everything.

Broderick collected his thoughts first. "There's something connecting Vincent, Malcolm, and Kiki."

I nodded. "With Kiki it could be anything because we know she runs her high-profile escort business. And we all know that her clientele is extensive. Speaking of, have either of you hired her?"

Both Damien and Broderick shook their heads, and I figured as much. At the very least she didn't have anything on the three of us unless someone told her some information.

I continued. "Good. My thinking is that the only way we might potentially be able to find out what Vincent was up to is by talking to Will. Damien, would you be okay setting that up?"

"Of course. Especially if it will bring closure to all the shit we're going through. Let me set something up and I'll get back to you."

"And if either of you come up with a suggestion that might explain the connection between those three, we are all ears."

Both of my brothers nodded and stood up almost at the same time. Broderick looked at me and said, "I know it might not seem like it all the time, but I think I can speak for Dad and Damien here and say that we are proud of you. It's obvious that you are serious about what it is you're doing right now, and we are glad to share the stage with you in representing all of the interests of our business, but more importantly, our family."

I nodded, not sure what to say in response. The two left without another word and I was left alone in the silence of my office to reflect.

20

MELISSA

I waited until after five thirty to knock on Gage's office door. I'd been stewing in my feelings for most of the day, wondering if he'd invited me to this work conference because of my job performance or my performance in the bedroom. My emotions shifted from being pissed to being happy that I had the opportunity to go to being pissed all over again. I'd worked too hard all of these years for my selection to go to this work conference to be a result of me lying on my back.

I knocked and waited for him to tell me to come in. When he did, I opened the door and barely caught it before it slammed closed.

"Did you ask me to go on this trip because we're having sex?"

A smirk appeared on his face, increasing the urge to throttle him. "I figured that would be a potential perk."

I took a step to storm over to him and give him a piece of my mind. Before I could take another, Gage spoke again. "The reason why I invited you on this work trip to Hawaii had to do with the work you've put in over the last few weeks. I've watched you as you've worked tirelessly to balance what is essentially two jobs. I think the experience that you would get there would be easily applied to what you're doing now, but more so to the management role you'll be in soon."

"Why didn't you just say that when I asked you?"

"Because watching you get angry is a huge fucking turn-on. Now come here."

I followed his directions, but when he pointed at his lap, I shook my head. "No way. I don't want anyone to come in here and see me sitting on your lap."

"Chances are no one would come in because it's after hours."

"And if someone does, they'll assume we are having an inappropriate relationship."

The smirk was back. "Well, technically."

"Shut up." It wasn't something I needed to be reminded about again.

Instead of sitting on his lap, I walked over to one of the chairs in front of his desk and took a seat. He bent down and pulled a bottle of tequila out from wherever its resting place was.

"Are you drinking on the job?"

He chuckled. "Hardly, and if I wanted to, who's going to tell me that I'm not allowed to?" He then produced two glasses. "I keep this in the office to celebrate some of our wins. Now is a good time to celebrate one of yours."

I watched as he poured the liquid into both glasses before handing one to me.

"To an amazing presentation and an amazing time in

Hawaii." He clanked his glass against mine and I took a small sip and let the liquor sit in my mouth.

"Swallow."

His demand sent a shock wave straight to my core. I did as he asked, allowing the alcohol to flow down my throat. There was a slight burn on the way down, but the warmth that came from it outweighed everything. I'd never quite tasted anything like it and who knew if I ever would again?

"Smooth, isn't it?"

I nodded but didn't take another sip. I hoped that this drink wouldn't make me intoxicated, but that should have been the furthest thing from my mind. After all, the man in front of me did that all on his own.

Gage stood up from his chair and came to stand in front of me. He gently removed the glass from my hand and placed both his and mine on the far corner of his desk.

He leaned down and kissed me, and before it could get too hot and heavy, he said, "I'm going to take you right here, where anyone who is left on this floor can hear you."

A surge of confidence pulsated through me because of the fleeting anger. "What took you so long?"

Although he lacked the finesse that he had at my home, he lifted me up and sat me on his desk. He pushed my legs apart and stepped between them before his lips smashed into my own. His kiss was urgent but mimicked my desire to have him take me.

"You know what I've been wondering?" he asked when he pulled away from me and whispered in my ear.

I shook my head and felt as he placed one of my dark curls behind my ear.

"What you're wearing beneath this dress. I haven't been

able to get the thought out of my mind especially while you were walking back and forth, explaining each item on the PowerPoint."

I sucked in a huge breath when he nibbled on my earlobe and when he soothed the place where he bit me with his tongue, I trembled under his touch. I held back the plea that was on my lips, the urge to beg him to take me right now was the only thing I could think about. He chuckled for a split second, and I knew he'd seen my reaction to his ministrations.

He moved slightly to look me in the eye as one of his hands moved from its position on the desk and landed on my knee. It only stayed there temporarily before it made its way up my inner thigh. The heat within me grew every inch his hand moved and soon he was leaving light, feathery touches on my pussy.

"This feels like lace...were you expecting something to happen tonight?"

"I don't wear nice underwear for you."

He shrugged and the smirk appeared. "You mean to tell me that when you were getting dressed this morning, pulling these flimsy panties up your smooth, pale legs that you weren't thinking of me, Melissa?"

I thought about lying but knew that wouldn't get me anywhere. Instead of waiting for my answer, he moved the thin piece of fabric out of the way so that he had complete access to me. Yet, he didn't move once he had.

"Tell the truth and you'll earn your *first* orgasm."

I shivered at his emphasis on 'first' and I was tired of waiting. "Fine, I put the panties on this morning and thought of you while I was doing so. Happy?"

"Very."

And then his finger eased into my center, making me breathe a sigh of relief. It took him no time to catch up to how fast I wanted him to go and then he stopped. A noise left my mouth in protest until he kneeled in front of me. Gage pushed my dress up and I lifted my hips so that he could slowly pull the fabric down my legs. He looked up at me, his eyes made darker by his desire before his face disappeared and I felt his breath on my exposed flesh. The first lick on my clit made me release an involuntary sigh and I leaned back on his desk, knocking into who knew what. Things would need to be picked up when we were done, but that wasn't something I needed to worry about right now.

He licked me again and I moaned, loving the feel of his tongue giving me the pleasure that I'd craved since he left my home a few days ago. The licking quickened and his fingers joined the mix, and my breathing grew heavier. It wouldn't be long before I reached the edge and I hoped he wouldn't play some sick game and stop the havoc he was wreaking all over my body. When I orgasmed, the tornado he'd caused in my body lessened, allowing me to finally breathe or so it felt.

He moved back and stood up, his gaze never straying from mine. His hands made their way toward my back. Without breaking eye contact, I helped him by grabbing my hair with one hand and pulling it toward the side, in hopes that it wouldn't get caught in the zipper. The only noise that was between us was my labored breathing after what his fingers and tongue had just done to my body. The dress pooled at my waist before I lifted my hips, allowing him to pull the dress off my body. I watched as he stared at me and noticed that I was wearing a bra that matched the panties that he'd snatched off. He reached into his pocket before removing his pants.

"I can't wait to take you without this." He lifted the foil packet in his hands so that I could see.

I held my breath when he ripped the packet. It was as if I was mesmerized by his actions as I watched him sheathe himself in the condom. He opened my legs that I hadn't realized drifted closed after our last adventure. He put his hands on my upper thighs and gently pushed my legs open so that he could step between them. He leaned down and kissed me, this time not as urgent, but more passionately, making my toes curl. It was the first time he'd kissed me in a while and I could feel his erection grow, impatiently waiting for showtime.

When the kiss ended naturally, I could hear how hard he was breathing. It was all just from a kiss, and it was fun to know that he was just as affected by that kiss as I was. His hand moved between us just before I felt his dick teasing at my entrance. A dry chuckle left his mouth when I gasped as he pushed into my pussy. My legs wrapped themselves around his waist and when he was fully seated in me, I let my head fall back.

"You don't know how stunning you look right now, in this very moment," he said.

I shuddered when I felt his finger run down my throat. He pulled out of me almost completely before he thrust into me. And then he did it again. And again.

I groaned when his movements became more consistent, less teasing. He lifted one of my legs so that it was resting on his shoulder and kissed the inside of my ankle before slamming into me. I cried out from the pleasure surging through my body.

"Yes. Tell everyone who is still here working late, what I'm doing to you."

I didn't care who knew as long as he kept pounding into my core, I couldn't care less about how much noise I was making. "Whatever you do, don't stop fucking me."

Gage grinned. "Sounds good, boss."

His movements sped up and the position allowed him to go deeper, earning moans from me and grunts from him. I knew I was getting close, and he must have known too because he sped up again and that was all it took.

My climax hit hard, causing me to shake around him and his grin widened. My orgasm does nothing but encourage him to keep going until he found his release as well, the low groan and the slowing of his movements indicating it.

He slowly removed my leg from his shoulder and leaned down to kiss me, ending our fucking with a slow luxurious kiss that I knew would stay on my mind for days to come. How had me storming into his office turned into this, I would never know, but I didn't regret it. Not one bit.

21

GAGE

When my personal phone rang on my desk, I grabbed it and looked at who was calling me during the workday. My eyes narrowed at the name that appeared on my screen. It couldn't be. Was it really...

"Gage," I said.

"Hey, man."

I was temporarily stunned. It was Ace Bolton, someone who's voice I hadn't heard in a long time. The last time I heard from him was at a reunion and fundraiser for Brentson University a few years back. When we were growing up, Broderick, Hunter and I were joined at the hip. As we got older, we all expanded our friend circles and as a result, I met Ace through some of the extracurriculars that we participated in.

There was a while there, though, that Ace and I had stopped hanging out as often. I regretted that and now I wondered why it had happened. Part of it was on me for not taking the time to get to the bottom of it.

When I'd seen him at the reunion we'd barely gotten to

chat, as he'd had to fly out again on assignment early the next morning. So to have him calling me now had me floored. "I'm shocked that you're calling me."

"Trust me, it's taken a long time to get to this point."

I ran a hand over my head. "Do I even want to ask what happened to you?"

"Probably not, but Kingston reached out to me when he told me you were digging deeper into Kiki.'

That made me sit up straighter. How had Kingston known how to get into contact with Ace? Why hadn't he told me if we were working together? Then again, could I blame him if I was keeping some of Kiki's discretions to myself? "Oh really?"

"Mmhmm."

"Do you want to meet up somewhere to chat? I'm going out of town tomorrow but am available tonight."

"No can do. Still on an assignment," Ace said. "But I've been meaning to get back at her since the shit she pulled when I was a kid."

"Shit she did to you as a kid?" I waited to see if he would confirm what I suspected he meant without me having to be the one to say it.

"She fucked me up. I'm still not completely over it and I'm not sure I'll ever be."

"She did it to you too." I couldn't bring myself to say the words.

Silence on the other end of the line confirmed my suspicions. "It went on for three years."

"Son of a—" It didn't take much to put together why she'd been able to get away with it. Ace's parents had died long before we'd met, and it wouldn't be a shock that she'd run into him at some point given the social circles we ran in. Why I'd thought I might have been the only one, I didn't know. It was also clear that he hadn't had anyone there to stop her preying. *Three fucking years?* I'd noticed he had become standoffish, but I had been dealing with my own shit at the time and had my head up my own ass.

"I want to apologize for not being there for you, but I know that wouldn't be enough now."

He snorted. "There was nothing you could do about it. But I do want to say that if you don't get to her first, she's mine and I will make sure that she pays for the pain that she has inflicted on my life."

I knew that he meant every word too. "You got it. What is it that you want to tell me?"

"Kingston mentioned that you were suspicious about how the charges against her were dropped. Within a few days of the announcement that Kiki was free to go, the prosecutor paid off all of the debt that he'd incurred."

"Are you talking about just student loan debt?"

"That, and his credit card debt and his house was paid off."

"But he's dead now. I remember reading in the news that he died maybe a year after Kiki was let go."

"Right and the reasoning was a 'heart attack'."

Ace's emphasis on heart attack told me that there was more to it than that. "And now based on what you're telling me, it sounds like it was anything but."

"Oh, it was a heart attack. But did it happen naturally is the question."

"Once we find out who it was that put the hit out on him, we'll know who set all of this into motion."

"And there you go. Happy to have helped and remember what I said about Kiki."

"You got it." I hung up the phone and leaned back in my chair, thinking about what Ace had told me. Before I could guilt trip myself some more, I dialed Kingston's number and waited for him to answer.

"What happened?" he asked instead of your stereotypical phone greeting.

"We'll talk about how you've been able to get in contact with Ace after all of this time later."

"He's done some work for me, and we've had to keep our connection quiet. For his safety and mine."

I could understand that. "Anyway Ace filled me in on what happened with the prosecutor, and I was thinking maybe we should try to track the money trail there. I don't want to go as far as to track his family members because more than likely it will lead to a wild goose chase, but if we have to take those measures, so be it."

"That's fine. I'll put some people on it as soon as I get off the phone.

22

GAGE

"I'm already tired and we just got here." She glared at me when I chuckled as I shut the door behind her. "It's lovely that my predicament is bringing you such joy."

That only made me laugh harder as I closed the door behind her. "You're hangry and we'll make sure you're properly fed soon. You're going to need your energy for one reason or another."

If my words weren't enough to let her know what I was referring to, the look I gave her should have been. It caused a change in the energy in the room as the mood shifted from lightheartedness to lust.

We arrived at our hotel on the Big Island about forty minutes ago. After we made it through the check-in process, Melissa went to her room to drop her things off and we agreed that she would come back to mine because it was larger. My plan was for her to spend most of her time in my room when we were not networking and attending conference events, but we'd agreed to keep the illusion that there was nothing personal going on between us just in case. I also got a slight thrill having her sneak into my room periodically anyway.

"Is there anything in particular you'd like to eat?"

She shrugged her shoulders, still looking around my room, probably comparing it to hers. Her hotel room could fit into this room at least twice, maybe even three times. It included its own kitchen and large windows that allowed you to see the beauty that was Hawaii.

I walked away from Melissa to order our dinner. It gave me a few seconds to look at her without her realizing. While she read over one of the pamphlets, I took my time watching her, the way her dark curls fell over her shoulders. They were begging for me to run a hand through them.

"Sir, I can take your order."

I rattled off my order without hesitation and then confirmed the small details and hung up so that I could quickly get back to Melissa.

"Dinner should be here soon," I said after I hung up the phone.

"Thank you."

I knew she would like what I selected. I'd watched what she'd ordered on the airplane and went from there when choosing dinner. I went with a surf and turf option on the menu and was proud of my choice. When there was a knock on the door sometime later, I walked over and opened it to let the waiter bring in our dinner. Once everything was signed and set up including the wine that I suspected she would like, the waiter let himself back out and I watched to see what Melissa would do. My grin grew wider when she saw what I ordered.

"How'd you know I would like this?"

I raised an eyebrow at her. "Was this some sort of test?"

She shook her head. "No, I truly didn't know what I wanted to eat. So, how'd you know?"

"I watched you. Watched what you like, what makes you shake your head in disgust or smile with glee. Although you think you're blending into the background by remaining quiet, your face is so expressive that it's easy to tell exactly what you need. But that's not all."

"Oh?"

I took a step toward her. "It's my job to know your wants, your needs, and your desires."

I meant every word, and she shivered slightly as I stared her down. I meant that more than anything I'd ever meant in my entire life. It had become a mission of mine to know all there was to know about her, and yet I still wanted to know more.

There was no doubt in my mind that there was still a lot she wasn't telling me. I thought back to how much was still missing from her file and why Dad had let that slip by. I hadn't talked to him much since our big blow up, but maybe that was a conversation that needed to happen if I couldn't get Melissa to talk to me. It wasn't an avenue I wanted to pursue because I wanted her to be the one that would fill me in on her life.

I brushed the back of my hand against her cheek before leaning down to kiss her. When I pulled away, I made a vow to myself that I would get to the bottom of whatever she was hiding if it was the last thing I did.

"This is delicious, thank you so much."

"You're welcome. And thank my father, he's paying for all of this."

Melissa's laughter was somewhat muffled because she was still trying to eat. I wanted to take her out to a lovely dinner, whether it be here or back home, and I just needed to figure out how. We'd settle into this unspoken relationship where we'd become each other's fuck buddies without asking too many questions and it was slowly driving me insane. I'd had plenty of one offs, or had been in casual relationships with other women, but it wouldn't fly with Melissa because I wouldn't allow it to. We ate in silence, enjoying our meal and the time we were spending with each other. Melissa spoke first.

"Do you need any help with your speech? I'm happy to listen to it if you like."

I stared at her for a moment trying to process her words because I hadn't been expecting that question. Her smile, which lit up her entire face, was genuine and held me back from telling her that I didn't need any help. I was invited to speak at this business conference as a way to encourage business leaders around the globe, but I didn't let on that I'd said a version of this speech multiple times before this. If she wanted to listen to the speech and help provide input on ways it could be changed or tweaked to make it better, then why not? After all, she'd done an excellent job on the PowerPoint presentation.

"Sure, how about after dinner? Then we should both get some rest."

She ate another forkful of food. "Sounds like a plan. After all, I'm already starting to feel jetlagged, but don't want to go to bed too early so that I can get accustomed to the time zone change."

"Funny. I know just the thing that can keep you awake."

"Of course you do." She took a napkin to wipe her lips. "Now are we going to get to the speech or what?"

"Who's to say that I was finished eating?"

"You, since you've been watching me eat for about a minute or two before I spoke up."

The feistiness made me chuckle and I laughed harder because it was true. I too used a napkin to wipe any crumbs from my face or hands and pushed my chair back. I grabbed my phone and stood up in front of the table almost like I was about to give a presentation before Melissa stopped me.

"Wait!" she exclaimed. She grabbed our wine glasses and said, "Let's move this to the living room."

I shook my head although I was happy to entertain her. We shifted our operations to the spacious living room. She placed the wine glasses down on the coffee table and hurried over to the sliding doors that opened onto a balcony. With the waves crashing outside, it truly felt as if we were in paradise for vacation and not a work conference.

"Okay, now you can begin. This is delicious by the way," she said, gesturing to the wine in her glass. I shook my head and stood up tall to make her giggle. It was time to get to work.

23

MELISSA

I joined everyone in giving Gage a standing ovation. He'd given a very rousing speech over the course of the last twenty-five minutes. I'd been engaged in his message and knew that it would resonate with others around the room. He'd worked hard on this speech, and it was evident given where he started and where the speech ended up. He talked about how he'd started several of his side ventures outside of Cross Industries and provided encouragement for others to do the same. When he recited the speech to me last night, I gave my opinion and he either readily made changes that I suggested, or we discussed it before he came to a decision. The hard work had clearly paid off as people were still clapping for him, and I couldn't help but smile.

I looked around the room to see how many people had come to listen to his speech and I had to estimate that there were at least three to four hundred people that had seats, several people had decided that they would rather stand than miss what Gage had to say and I assumed that at some point the speech would be uploaded on the internet. The thought of how many people that Gage could eventually be inspiring made goosebumps appear on my arms.

I hoped he was proud of his accomplishment and turned to look in his direction. The applause finally died down as Gage gave me the biggest smile when our eyes met. I returned the grin.

The change that I noticed in the short amount of time that I'd been working for him was fascinating. It was as if the cloud he'd been under had lifted and he'd stepped up to the plate to be more of a leader. I knew I'd had a part in helping him get to this point, including taking more of the administrative tasks off his plate, so I'd hoped that when it came time for my performance review that would all be considered.

My thoughts drifted to how life might be different once the transition into my new role took place. Would I be brought in to help search for both Damien and Gage's new assistants? I'd be happy to teach whomever it was the ropes and help make the transition to their new role more manageable. After all, I would say that since I've been helping Gage, things have been going well and I haven't heard any complaints from anyone.

More importantly, what would become of my relationship with Gage once I moved on to the new role?

Some laughter brought me out of my thoughts, and I looked over to find Gage talking to a woman and a man who'd stopped him when he stepped off the stage. Should I walk over there and join in on the conversation? No, I didn't want to interrupt them. It might be some time before he made his way back to me, so I started gathering my things, making a mental note of what work I had to do when I got a chance to sit down in front of my computer.

"Melissa, it's been a while."

I froze, immediately recognizing the man's voice. My eyes darted around the room, wondering if I could find an exit to get out of here. After all, this was an auditorium and I'd assume that there needed to be many exits in case of an emergency. In my mind, this qualified as such an event. What was the likelihood that I would run into him at this conference? There was no way he could be here, could he? I left him in Ohio and that was where he was supposed to stay.

"Calvin Rupert." The distaste I had for him was evident. He didn't look too terrible for someone who I'd hoped was rotting in hell.

"So you do know how to speak. It seems that every time I contacted you, you would—"

I stood up straight and squared my shoulders. Although I was petrified, I wouldn't let him see it. "I have nothing to discuss with you."

Calvin laughed. "Oh, we have plenty to discuss including you handing over that USB drive."

"It will be a cold day in hell before I ever give you that," I hissed at him. My heart was pounding loudly in my ears, and I worried that he'd hear it and think it a sign I was bluffing, but I wasn't. I wouldn't be giving up that USB drive to anyone.

"You'll be regretting that comment in another minute—" he started to threaten, but then suddenly stood up straight and took a step back, a pleasant smile crossing his face.

I gave him a confused look, until I felt a hand on my hip.

"Can I help you?"

I glanced at Gage out of the corner of my eye. I don't think

I'd ever been so happy to see him than I was right at that very moment.

Calvin held out his hand to shake. "I should probably introduce myself. My name is Calvin Rupert. Melissa and I go way back, and I was saying hello to her. After all, it's been a long time since we've seen each other."

"Gage Cross," he said as he shook Calvin's hand.

Their handshake made my skin crawl, and I gave an involuntary shiver that I knew Gage felt, since his left hand was still resting on my hip. I couldn't stand the thought of Calvin anywhere near me, but I felt slightly better having Gage here. If he wasn't, I'd be on the next flight home, debating whether it would be worth leaving New York City. Then again, this was a great opportunity for me, and I didn't want fuck that up. I wasn't going to let Calvin ruin my life again.

Calvin reached into his pocket and pulled out two pieces of paper. I assumed they were his business cards. He handed one to Gage and then to me. I refused to take it, instead looking at it with disgust. He tried to save face by quickly putting it back in his wallet, but the irritation in his expression was still there and I had a feeling that if it weren't for Gage being here, this would go a lot differently. When he was done, he turned his attention back to me.

"I didn't expect to see you here, Melissa, but we should catch up. It would be nice to hear what you've been up to after all these years."

"Fat chance of that."

Gage looked at me after my outburst and gave me a look that told me he was going to ask me about what this was all about later. I didn't want to deal with that.

Calvin seemed temporarily taken aback by my comment, but that didn't stop a slimy grin from appearing on his face.

Gage took a step closer to me before he said, "It's clear that Melissa doesn't want to talk to you, so why don't you run along?"

Calvin's gaze shifted between Gage and me before landing on Gage.

"It was lovely seeing you again, Melissa. Gage, I'm sure we'll talk soon."

"I bet we will."

Without saying anything else, Calvin left us to stand there watching as he walked away. I knew that it wouldn't be the last that I saw of him because I owned the one thing that he wanted most in this world.

24

GAGE

"I can't help you unless you tell me what's going on."

"Gage, I didn't ask for your help and it's a whole lot of stuff that you don't need to be involved in."

"Try me."

Melissa looked over at me across the table. She looked stunning in the soft light of the sunrise. She dragged me out of bed early in the morning to see the sunrise at least once when we were in paradise, even if it was for work. Instead of responding, she stared down into the cup of coffee that I served her just moments ago.

"Melissa, tell me what he did to you."

She lifted her gaze to meet mine and said, "He didn't do anything to me physically."

"That wasn't what I asked. Why did he approach you this afternoon?"

"I'll tell you, but first, you almost sound jealous."

I scoffed. "Hardly." That was a lie, but I wasn't jealous for the reason she thought. I'd been wanting to know more about her, and it seemed that he had intimate knowledge of a major event that took place in her life that I didn't. "It was because I could see that you were in distress. That's all."

"Because you watch me."

"Exactly."

Melissa sighed and ran a hand through her hair. It was easy to see that this wasn't something she really wanted to discuss, and I felt a hint of guilt at making her do so. But if getting to the bottom of this would in the end help her, it was worth it.

"He's a predator, but not in the way you'd expect. He tried to force my mother to sell her home to him and I put my foot down so it didn't happen."

"How?"

Melissa didn't say anything, but her face did. Her lip trembled just before she bit it, as she tried to keep her expression neutral but failed. I reached over, grabbed her hand, and gently rubbed it.

"Mom had an early onset of dementia, and it was almost as if one moment she was fine and the next she wasn't. With that came a lot of stressors on me as I was forced to take over her affairs and try to make sure things were straightened out before...she would pass on."

I opened my arms and gestured for her to come over and sit on my lap. When she did, I wrapped my arms around her, wishing that this would be an easy fix for the pain that she was reliving.

"It was so hard to watch her deteriorate right before my eyes. One day she'd recognize me, the next day she wouldn't. If she hadn't made me promise to go to NYU on one of her more lucid days, I would have stayed in Ohio to make sure that her affairs were in order."

"What happened to your home and where does Calvin fit into the picture?"

"Sold it to a lovely family that I hope is still enjoying it. Calvin tried to play on my mother's heart strings and get her to marry him so that not only could he get her money, but the house as well. I was a thorn in Calvin's side because I shut all of that shit down and I didn't give him the win he desired and the files I have on him prove it. Letters and voice memos that I was able to record when he thought that no one else was listening while he was supposed to be the loving and attentive boyfriend to my mom would lead to the end of him. If I went to the media with what I know, he would be castrated by the public. Back then, he was trying to make waves in politics, and I assume that's what he's trying to do now. He also had a lot of friends in high places so any of this coming out would mean that I had a target on my back if I went back there. I essentially did my best with what I had to keep a low profile and he didn't bother me for years. Until now."

I'd bet that he was still trying to do that and had bigger ambitions than just being known as a business. That became problematic if Melissa had evidence of how he tried to bulldoze a sickly woman and her young daughter into selling her home to him. And why was he coming after her now, after all these years?

Having her confirm my thoughts about there being more here than met the eye made me feel as if I was on the edge of a huge discovery. I'd had Dave dig deeper into her background, and he'd shed a little more light on what Melissa had gone through, but not as much as I was hoping. This allowed me to put some of the pieces together and get to know the woman behind this organized exterior.

The more Melissa spilled her heart to me, the guiltier I felt. I wanted to tell her about the night at Kiki's, but something was preventing me from doing so. I didn't know if it was self-preservation for myself or for her. I knew that telling her what I knew about the first time we were together would lead to more turmoil she shouldn't have to deal with. I also knew it would change our relationship, and not for the better. That wasn't something I was willing to risk.

"I'm going to take him down."

"You're going to what?"

"He will be taken care of. This is none of your concern anymore."

Her head swerved and she stared at me. "What do you mean this is none of my concern? I've been living in fear of this man for years and I—"

"And that won't be a problem for you anymore. Trust me."

I could see the uneasiness in her eyes before her gaze hardened. "Gage, you can't just bulldoze over my thoughts and opinions. You won't."

"That isn't what I'm doing. I'm taking care of a situation that I know I can make better. You won't have to worry about Calvin anymore. And that's final."

I could see that she wanted to fight me on this, but that was the last thing she needed to do. I made a promise to her to rectify this situation as soon as possible, hopefully resolving a years-long conflict and bringing her some peace. But something told me that there was more to this than met the eye.

I needed to be careful with how I did things. Melissa

could be defiant if she wanted to, and I didn't want to chase her out of my life or have an incident where she ended up in harm's way. Then again, if she found out what I was hiding, there was probably no chance in hell that she would stick around anyway.

25

MELISSA

A couple of weeks later I found myself walking into Elevate, the bar and sex club that the Cross brothers owned. It felt weird walking in here on Gage's arm, but he hadn't wanted it any other way. I assumed no one here outside of his family would know who I was, but the prospect of someone seeing me did have me freaking out a bit. That was in addition to this being the first time that Gage and I were in public together.

As soon as we walked up to where Damien, Anais, Broderick, and a striking blonde who was standing to his left, Broderick swore. "I knew it."

"If you want to still have your good looks, you'll stop—"

Broderick raised an eyebrow. "You think I look good?"

"Yes, because I look fantastic, and we know that I took most of the looks in the womb."

I cracked a smile as the brothers joked with one another. It was lovely to see Gage in a more relaxed setting, and it wasn't surprising that his family would put him in one. Although it was clear how hard they worked to make Cross

Industries into the enigma that it was, they also played just as hard and tried to relax when the time called for it.

Speaking of playing hard, my nerves were abuzz due to us being in a sex club, even though we were all standing in the VIP area. I thought back to the adventure that I'd had at Kiki's party, and the same thrill that shot through my body there had returned. Gage had explained to me some of the aspects of what occurred downstairs, and I couldn't wait to explore it myself. Sex with Gage was phenomenal but exploring a new place with him would be all the more magical.

We were interrupted when we were each handed a glass of champagne. Damien looked at each person in our group before he held up his glass. The rest of us followed and he said, "This club wouldn't be where it is today if it wasn't for these two here. Congratulations on taking this place to heights that even I didn't imagine."

We all clinked our glasses together and took a sip of the champagne in them. It took a few minutes but when Anais finished drinking from her glass, she turned to me. "I'm so grateful for all that you did to help us pull off our fake engagement...that turned into a real engagement."

I couldn't help but smile. It was easy to see how in love they were, and it warmed my heart. "It was nothing."

"Nonsense. I know it took a lot of effort." She paused before her eyes widened and a smile appeared on her face. "You know what, why don't I organize a spa day for you?"

"Oh, that's too much."

"Nonsense. I'll see what I can pull together. I want to show my gratitude."

I couldn't lie to myself and say that a spa day wouldn't be

wonderful, so instead of fighting it, I nodded my head. "Sounds like a great idea."

Anais clapped her hands together. "Fantastic. I'll get everything squared away and will reach out about your availability."

I smiled in return and turned my head as another woman approached our group.

"Ellie!" Anais exclaimed as she made her way to the newcomer. She turned back to face the rest of us before looking back at Ellie and saying, "Everyone, this is Ellie, my best friend. Melissa might be the only person you don't know?"

Ellie nodded. "That sounds about right. I met Grace, Broderick, and Gage at your engagement party if I'm remembering correctly."

Grace smiled before turning toward her boyfriend. "Yes, just before Broderick decided to act like an asshole."

Broderick looked at the blonde next to him and slid his arm to where no one could see it. I assumed it landed on Grace's ass given how she jumped and then tapped him on the chest.

I grinned at their interaction and turned to Gage, who hadn't said much since Anais asked me about the spa day. I found him looking down at me. He didn't say anything, but I could feel the heat in his stare, warming me all over. My thoughts once again floated the idea of what was going to occur once we eventually made our way to the basement. It was then that I realized that I had no idea what I was getting myself into outside of what I had read about in passing or seen on television. This would be a completely new experience, and I was entrusting my passion and desire in him. I trusted him, and that wasn't what I expected when I talked myself into joining this adventure. How the tides had changed.

A clearing of the throat drew our attention to the person who had interrupted us. I'd recognized him but couldn't place him. A quick glance to my right showed that Ellie wasn't happy to see him.

"Kingston! Nice of you to join us." Damien was the first one to greet him. It was then when it clicked, because his name was more familiar to me than his face. Kingston was the Cross brothers' older cousin who ran the security firm that was securing Cross Industries more thoroughly. I should have noted the family resemblance. He didn't closely resemble Damien and his twin brothers, but it was easy to see that they were related.

"Happy to be here," Kingston said, and his eyes were trained on Ellie. She exaggerated an eye roll and turned her attention to Anais, who was still standing next to her. I looked at Gage, who looked back at me and shrugged.

Kingston then spoke again. "I came here to celebrate with you, but also wanted to talk to Gage for a moment."

Gage squeezed my hand before leaving with Kingston. I watched as the two men walked away and took another sip from my glass. Before either one of the men looked at me and found me staring at them, I turned my attention back to the group. It was then that I noticed that Damien had moved and was standing next to me.

"How is everything going?"

I shrugged. "I can't complain. Balancing your schedule sometimes with Gage's has been a challenge, but other than that, things are going well."

"And the trip to Hawaii?"

The mention of the trip made me smile. I decided not to dwell on what had happened when Gage and I ran into Calvin. "Wonderful. Watching Gage speak was uplifting."

"He really knows how to tie some lighthearted humor into the message he's trying to get across."

"That's it. Also watching him work the room and getting to meet so many people was great."

"And I'm sure the location couldn't be beat."

The gleam in Damien's eye made it easy to see where he was going with this conversation, but I wasn't about to take the bait. "Hawaii was stunning, and I hope to visit it again some day.

"That's good. I wasn't completely expecting him to bring you tonight."

I raised an eyebrow at his shift in topic. Now he wasn't looking at me. "But you had some inclination that he would?"

Damien nodded. "Broderick and I suspected that something was going on between the two of you after he invited you on the work trip."

I shrugged but didn't give anything more. Damien had a way of picking up on someone's nervousness and turning it into an advantage for himself, and I didn't want that to be the case here. "I'm happy to be here to celebrate this accomplishment with you all."

I knew my answer sounded very professional and that was because I felt as if my back were up against the wall. Here I was, standing in a bar, above a sex club, talking to the man who was sort of my boss. On top of that, I was attending this celebration with his younger brother, who was also my boss, and now he knew we were sleeping together. *Awkward* didn't begin to describe it.

As if he were reading my thoughts, Damien said, "No need to think that I'm trying to attack you. Whatever is going on between you and Gage is your business, not mine, and there's nothing in our policies that says you shouldn't be dating. However, I wouldn't be surprised if something like that does end up in there now."

I did a double take. "Why is that?"

"Dad will more than likely see it as a liability. It hasn't come up as far as we know before, or at least the parties involved made sure that whatever they were doing, didn't carry on into the workplace."

I nodded my head as I digested the information. So, if we continued to keep this "thing" under wraps, then everything should be fine. Gage and I hadn't talked about what our relationship with one another would look like outside of fucking each other's brains out, so that would be fine by me.

I could feel Gage looking at me before I heard him interrupt our conversation. The hairs on the back of my neck stood up when I felt his hand land along my lower back just before he pulled me close to him, anchoring me to his side as if he was protecting me from his brother. The quizzical look that I knew covered my face couldn't be stopped, and when Gage looked down at me, he said nothing, refusing to offer an explanation as to why he was behaving this way.

Damien smirked but didn't comment on what had just unfolded in front of him. Anais strolled up to him, dragging his attention away from Gage and me. Gage used that opportunity to his advantage.

"Excuse us," he said as he loosened his grip on me and

steered my body toward the exit. He then grabbed my hand so that I would follow him toward the stairs.

"What's the big hurry? Don't you want to say goodbye to everyone else?"

I didn't know if he'd heard me until he replied, "Nope."

Before he could get to the stairs, I was able to pull my hand out of his grasp, forcing him to stop. It didn't make him turn around to face me, however. "What you're going to do is talk to me as if I'm a person and not drag me around like I'm some lost puppy."

He still didn't turn around.

My frustration grew as I stared at his back. The black button-down shirt fit him perfectly and I longed to open each button painfully slowly, causing him to feel the same amount of frustration that I was feeling currently.

"Are you going to talk to me about what put you in this funky mood or what?"

This time he did turn around, giving me the opportunity to stare into his dark brown gaze.

"I'm going on another business trip."

That hadn't been what I was expecting. "You're going on another trip?" I wished he would take me with him, but there was no way I was saying that out loud.

Gage nodded. "Nowhere near as fun, however."

"And that is enough to piss you off?"

"Yes," he said as his stride ate up the distance between the two of us. "Because it's taking me away from you." He leaned down and placed a light kiss on my lips. "To make up for the time I'll be gone, we're heading down to the basement."

I nodded, understanding why he was in the rush he was in now. He took my hand once again and instead of pulling me along, we walked to the stairs side by side. There was no way in hell I was going to turn back around and look at the group we'd left, because I didn't want to see the looks that they were undoubtedly giving to us.

"Don't I need some kind of pass to get into the basement?"

"Don't worry, I have everything you need."

In more ways than one.

26

GAGE

I led Melissa down a dark hallway, much like I'd done that evening at Kiki's. A sense of déjà vu clouded my mind and took over my thoughts as we traveled to the room that I selected for us. Desperation soon took its place as I thought about how I hadn't come clean to her about who I was when we first fucked. I needed to tell her about that, that way we could move past it and move on with our lives.

I walked all the way to the end of the hallway, and we stood in front of a door. I gave her a smile before I opened the door, and we entered a world where only she mattered. It was something I was hoping to make more permanent than just fucking whenever we want, but it wasn't the right time for that conversation.

She gasped when she looked at our surroundings, and I closed the door behind us. I'd chosen a room that looked like your stereotypical bedroom, but it had one special feature: a sex swing.

"Are we going to be using that?"

"That's the plan." I walked up behind her and shifted her

curls out of my way. I leaned down and kissed her neck. I nibbled on the place I'd just kissed and moved my hands so that I could unzip the dress that had been teasing me all night.

"It's probably easier for you to pull the dress over my head." As she said that, she pulled the dress over her head in one motion.

I let my eyes roam down her body, enjoying the sight before me. But I wanted to get my hands on her body now. The thong she had on showcased her ass perfectly and I couldn't wait to grab a handful of her ass as I pounded into her while she was suspended on that swing.

She switched it up tonight with a matching lacy lavender bra and panty set and I walked around her to get an eyeful of how she looked tonight. Her body looked delectable, and I couldn't wait to not only enjoy her body tonight, but make sure it was pleasurable for her as well.

My eyes stared at her lips, which were begging to be kissed and I had no problem obliging. When she parted her lips, I snuck my tongue in to explore her mouth, making sure to show her how my mouth was going to devour her in just a few minutes.

I felt her hand slide between us and start fumbling with the button down I'd worn, eager to strip it off my body. I wanted to feel her tits against my bare chest as much as she did. We broke apart when I needed to take off my shirt, but I was back on her almost immediately. My hands made their way to her breasts and instead of unsnapping her bra, I shifted the bra cups to the side and bent down and licked her nipple once. Twice. Then I put her nipple in my mouth as her hand made its way into my hair.

The moan that left her lips vibrated through my body and made my dick twitch. I shifted my attention to her other breast, lavishing it with licks and nibbles that I knew would make her wet. My hand drifted down her body and found the waistband of her underwear and then an idea came to me.

"Pull your panties down your legs and step out of them."

She looked as if she might argue with me, but she didn't, instead choosing to follow directions.

"Do you want to wear those shoes in the swing?"

She shook her head and stepped out of them. I kissed her again and backed her into where the swing was set up. Once she was settled in the swing, I kneeled in front of her and put my mouth on her pussy.

"Oh my—" Her words were cut off when I sucked on her clit. I looked up at her and found her with her eyes closed just before her head fell back. I loved watching her come apart for me.

When I inserted a finger into her core, she asked, "What are you doing to me?"

"Driving you wild."

"I'm already going to—" Her words stopped suddenly when she found her release and I couldn't help but smirk at her current state.

I made her this way, and I couldn't be more proud.

She was still breathing heavily when she looked at me, her eyelids looked as if she couldn't open them up all the way. When my hand touched my belt, she said, "I don't want to use condoms tonight."

Thank fuck. "I'm clean."

"As am I. And on birth control."

I looked at her sitting in the swing and felt my cock twitch again. Without any more prompting, I pushed into her, enjoying the little moans she made as I slid in. Inch by inch.

When we started moving, I couldn't help but watch her tits jiggle with each motion. I could tell that the angle that the swing put her in was perfect because every time I moved, she gasped. Any attempt to catch her breath after her first orgasm went out the window.

"Gage."

I watched as she bit her lip, wanting nothing more than to kiss her again.

"Fuck," I mumbled under my breath as I closed my eyes, enjoying the sensation of her pussy on my cock. I knew it would feel great with no barrier between us, but I hadn't counted on it feeling this amazing.

Foolish of me, I know.

I found my rhythm and slammed into her harder, her moans and groans encouraging me to continue what I was doing, and I had no problem with that. I placed my hands on her ass, allowing me to go even deeper into her. When she clamped down on me, I groaned, loving the feel and knowing that once again, she was close to her peak. I sped up my thrusting and soon she came apart in my arms. While she rode out her orgasm, I continued pounding into her until I found mine, the only thing I could hear was the pounding of my heart in my ears.

While I tried to slow my racing heart, Melissa looked up at me and grinned. "I'll never look at a swing the same way again."

27

MELISSA

I groaned as I felt the tension in my shoulders leave my body. I couldn't remember the last time I'd had a massage, but this felt glorious. I was thankful to Anais for thinking of this because I didn't know how much I needed this self-care opportunity until I was experiencing it.

Anais had set up this whole experience in the penthouse that had been the scene of her and Damien's fake engagement announcement shoot. I'd been to the penthouse a handful of times but lying on this masseuse table in the guest room was much different than the chaos that was surrounding the room while we tried to get everything ready for the announcement. The sounds of the soft music that played in the background and the now dimly lit guest room had set the mood and provided a relaxing experience.

"I'll leave you here to change and Anais has another surprise for you in the living room."

I nodded slightly, letting Ellie know that I heard her, but my body didn't want to move just yet. The state of bliss that I was in would be ruined if I made any motions and I wasn't ready to give that up.

If someone had said that Ellie's hands were magical, I would've believed them. She had my body in such a state of relaxation that I thought that if I sat up right now, I would turn to mush.

When I knew there was no way that I could prolong the inevitable, I got up from the chair and threw on my T-shirt and yoga pants. When I left the room, I couldn't help but smile due to how at ease I felt even though before I got here, I felt as if my world was spinning out of control.

Gage left last night to go on the last-minute out-of-town trip, so it was the first time in a while that my life was back to where it had been before he had stormed in headfirst. It felt strange to not see him walk by me when he came into the office or have us enter the building from separate entrances in order to hide the fact that we'd arrived together. We'd been in touch since he'd been gone, but it wasn't the same.

When I walked out into the living room, I was greeted by a sight I hadn't expected. Ellie had changed her clothes and now both she and Anais were in the living room with what looked like a nail salon set up. There were two nail technicians standing by as well.

"Okay, this is officially way too much. There is no way that I can accept all of this," I said as I took everything in.

Anais shrugged. "Then just think of it as me being selfish and having this whole setup done for me and you just happen to be here. Come on."

I chuckled as one of the technicians gave me a big grin before gesturing that I should follow her. Once I'd picked out a bright red color for my nails, I sat down in my chair and got comfortable as the session began.

"Do you want a glass of lemon water? We also have wine because Damien keeps this place stocked for when we stay here."

"Lemon water would be great," I said. It would be nice to have something refreshing after my nails were done.

Anais grabbed the drinks and placed one near me before she sat down in the makeshift station next to mine. Ellie grabbed her own and sat in another chair. I must have sent her a curious look because she said, "I might get a pedicure, but I usually don't do too much to my nails due to the massages."

My mouth opened into an 'O' as I nodded my head. I knew I probably looked silly, but I hadn't thought of that being a reason.

"It was so great running into you at the party the other night."

I looked over at Anais and couldn't help but smile back at her. Her entire demeanor was cheerful, and while I knew that we all had our issues, she had a lot to be happy about.

"I was happy to be there, even if it felt weird due to my job." I looked at the technicians before I looked back at her. I didn't want to say out loud that it was strange to attend because Gage was technically my boss due to the strangers in the room. It might have been me being paranoid but given how well known the Cross family was in New York City, who knew what would get dragged out into the public sphere.

Anais gave me a look before she said, "I could see that given the circumstances of everything."

I was grateful that she seemed to have picked up on my being vague. "Yeah, but I had a great time."

Anais's smile turned into a smirk. "I bet you did. We all saw how quickly he whisked you off to go downstairs."

I could feel my cheeks heating up and I wanted to curse my fair skin.

"And left Kingston to stay with us," Ellie grumbled.

"What was up with that anyway? Why do you hate him?" I was happy to shift the attention off of me and onto anyone else.

"*Hate* is a strong word."

Anais rolled her eyes playfully. "But that is what you do. You can't stand him."

Ellie shrugged. "He's pissed me off ever since he stopped me from getting into the basement of Elevate by saying that we needed a coin or something."

"We need something like that now," Anais mumbled under her breath.

"You showed me the key. Anyway, he's been annoying me ever since." She then turned to me and said, "I live downstairs, and I see him sometimes around here and he tries to strike up conversations with me."

"Oh, the horror."

It was entertaining watching Anais and Ellie interact, and it was easy to see that they'd been friends forever. It was something I wished I had, and it was the first time in a long time that I had felt that way. I'd made it my mission to not maintain super close relationships with people out of fear. My relationship with Nia was fine, but there was plenty that she didn't know about me. I needed to get better at letting people in.

Much like I had let Gage in.

I looked at the two women in front of me, grateful for what I thought was the beginning of a beautiful friendship.

∽

That evening, after spending the afternoon with Anais and Ellie, I hung out on my couch, refusing to move as a result of my whole relaxation day. At least until my phone rang. I picked it up and smiled when I saw the name that appeared.

"Hello, Gage."

"What are you wearing right now?"

I giggled. "We're not doing this."

"I still control your pleasure no matter where I am. What are you wearing?"

I debated lying and saying that I was wearing something sexier than I had on but decided that honesty was the best policy. "I'm in a tank top and yoga pants."

"Good. I had something delivered to your apartment in a red bag. Why don't you go pick it up? Call me back once you've gotten it and read the letter."

"What did you—" But I heard nothing on the other end of the phone. With a heavy sigh, I stood up and walked to my front door. There was a bag sitting outside my door that hadn't been there when I got back from hanging out with Anais and Ellie.

If Gage hadn't told me that he'd sent the package, I might have been tempted to call the police because I didn't trust that Calvin wasn't trying to find another way to get me to turn over the USB. I closed my door behind me and walked over to my couch. The first thing I pulled out was a notecard and a quick skim of what was written on it made me laugh and aroused at the same time.

Melissa,

I wish I could be there to help complete your relaxing day, but this is the next best thing. Inside you'll find a couple of things that I want you to use this evening. Call me when you're ready. You're in for a real treat.

Gage

The last time I'd pulled out items from a gift bag, it was a mask and a wig for the party at Kiki's. Now, who knew what I was about to pull out of this bag that Gage had someone deliver to my home. I took a deep breath before I dipped my hand into the bag. What I pulled out first was wrapped in tissue paper. It took a bit of maneuvering, but I was able to open the package and found a burgundy bra and panty lingerie set. The set was beautiful, and I assumed it was made of silk. If I had to guess. When I reached to grab my phone to call Gage back, I knocked the bag over and something else fell out. It was a long velvety box that was the same color as the lingerie set. I picked it up from the floor and opened it.

He couldn't be serious, could he? Since I now had an idea about what tonight entailed, I walked over to my kitchen sink to wash the apparatus in the velvet box. When I placed the device back in the box and walked back into the living room, I called him back and waited for him to answer.

"Are you on your back with your legs open?"

"No, I—"

"So, you didn't follow my directions." The disapproval in his voice was evident.

"I—give me a second."

I grabbed everything and dashed into my bedroom. I

threw off my clothes and replaced them with the expensive lingerie Gage bought for me. When I took my hair out of the messy ponytail I'd put it in after I showered, I took a moment to admire the women staring back in the mirror at me. I looked fierce and ready for whatever the world was about to throw at me, including Gage Cross wanting to partake in phone sex. I shook my head and watched as my curls shifted on my shoulders.

I walked over to my bed and put the phone on speaker before laying back down on the bed. "I'm ready."

"Excellent, Sweetheart. How wet did you become when you opened the red velvet box?"

I bit the corner of my lip before I replied. "So wet. I can't wait to use it."

"In due time. First, I want you to massage your breasts through that pretty burgundy bra."

My hands made their way to my breasts, grabbing one of each and I massaged them while imagining it was his hands on me. A low moan left my lips.

"Already moaning for me?"

I made a noncommittal noise as my eyes drifted close and I embraced the feeling of my touch until Gage's voice cut through my thoughts.

"Move the cups out of the way so that your tits spill out. How hard are your nipples?"

I did as he asked and was pleased to find that my nipples were as hard as pebbles. They felt as if they wanted to be licked, but I knew that wouldn't be happening tonight. One of my hands drifted down my torso before reaching back up to my breast. He hadn't given me direction on when to stop handling my breasts, so it was best that I did as he asked.

"You don't know how much I wish I was there with you right now."

The feeling was mutual although I didn't voice that opinion because I was too busy wrapped up in my own little world.

"Now, I want you to place your index finger in your mouth and drag it down your body until you end up outside of that pretty pussy.

"I want you to coat your finger in your juices before you fuck yourself."

I swallowed hard as my other hand moved the panties out of the way and I let my finger swirl in my juices. My wetness clouded my judgement and I gasped when my finger entered my pussy.

"Fuck, you sound so sweet, and I know you taste just as delicious as the sounds coming out of your mouth."

"I wish this was you here fucking me."

I heard a moan come from the other end of the phone and that energized me. My pace grew faster as I hoped to find my release and by the sounds of it, Gage was trying to do the same. I imagined his hand on his cock, jerking up and down as he wished it were me slamming down on his dick.

"Don't forget the present I bought you. Use it now."

With the grace of a newborn giraffe, I reached over and grabbed the box and snatched the vibrator and its remote out of it. I put the toy on my clit and used the remote that came with it to turn it on. The vibrations sent me to another planet, away from all the troubles and stressors that I'd been dealing with and into a world where the only thing that mattered was me getting off. I heard Gage say something, but I couldn't figure out what it was over the sounds of the toy and me reaching my climax. I sang his praises as I came down off of the high and heard him groan as he followed me.

"Fuck, baby. That was hot."

I giggled, enjoying my post-climax glow and the feeling that him calling me baby gave me.

Gage continued, "Next time we need to do it with the camera on. But I can't say I didn't love imagining how you looked as you came."

How did he still have the ability to make me blush? I was grateful that there wasn't a camera on me because I'd probably turned the same shade as the lingerie I was wearing.

28

GAGE

I read over everything that Kingston sent me on Calvin and everything that Melissa had told me checked out. I decided to make the trip here at the last minute to surprise him on his turf. This scumbag was the lowest of the low, but I was willing to let him off with a warning for now. After all, he didn't live in New York City so it would be more difficult to pull any stunt, especially if he was still so hard up for cash that he was willing to commit fraud involving a woman who wasn't of sound mind.

Speaking of cash, I reviewed the financials that Kingston pulled on him and found that he had no debt to speak of anymore. Where had he gotten his money from? Some more reviewing showed that it all disappeared rather quickly. I was already calling Kingston before I could process what I was reading.

"Kingston."

"Did you review Calvin's files?" I skimmed the page I had open on my laptop again to make sure that my thoughts were correct.

"Not yet. I sent them over to you as soon as possible because you'd flown out to Ohio to meet with him. What did you find?"

"The debt that he was supposedly in? Gone."

Kingston didn't say anything for a beat. "All of it?"

"All of it."

"Any idea of who it might have been?"

I thought about it for a second. "Melissa mentioned that he had friends in high places out here so maybe they could have bailed him out."

I could hear Kingston typing on his keyboard. "That is a possibility."

I closed my eyes briefly as I tried to connect the dots for something that didn't seem to have dots to collect. Suddenly they sprung open, and I was grasping my phone for dear life. "Kingston."

"What did you just think of?"

"This might be far-fetched so just bear with me."

"Wouldn't be the first time."

I would have chuckled if it wasn't for the amount of pressure I was under. "Did we ever find anything on the prosecutor who dropped the charges against Kiki?"

"Nope. Any trace of the money that he received is long gone. His wife and kid live pretty modestly for New York City standards and that could be due to any life insurance policy or savings that he might have had."

"What if there is a connection between Calvin and the prosecutor? Someone paid them both off to carry out the shit they are doing?"

"That is pretty out there, Gage."

"My gut tells me something is up."

Kingston sighed. "Okay. Let me do some digging into Calvin and see if there might have been a slip up there. After all, at least he's not dead...yet."

"Good. Let me know if you find anything." And with that, I ended the call. I gathered the things I needed and stood up. A quick check of the time told me that if I headed out now, I would make my private flight back to New York City without any problems, but if I waited too long, it might cause an issue with having to reschedule things. I left the hotel room that I'd stayed in for the last few evenings and walked to the car that was mine while I was in Ohio.

Newham, Ohio wasn't the small town I was expecting. As I drove through the town, what should have been a charming place, was clouded by the ordeal that Melissa had to face before she left for college. I wanted her to be able to come back to her hometown if she wanted to and visit without the fear of something happening to her. If Calvin had no problem traveling all the way to Hawaii to attempt to confront her, then there was no telling what else he might try to pull. That was why I was here.

The drive to the address I had on file for Calvin didn't take too long and it was easy to find parking near where I had to go. I put the black sedan that I rented at the airport into park and looked up at the building in front of me. It was a two-family home that I assumed had been turned into a living area on the top floor while an office was on the main floor.

I walked up the porch steps and knocked on the door. While I waited for someone to answer, I looked around and noticed how homey the outside of the home looked. Who would have thought that some one as vengeful as Calvin would have lived here? Part of me wondered if this house was bought with any of the money that Melissa's Mom was supposed to have. I glanced at a car as it drove down the street and it was then that I finally heard a door unlock. I wasn't shocked when Calvin answered the door himself.

"Cross. Surprised that you flew all the way out here to pay me a visit." He moved to the side to let me in but didn't offer to let me walk further into the house. That was just fine by me.

"Trust me, it was no problem. It is nice to see you too, Calvin." That was a bold-faced lie. I wanted to deck him, but I refrained.

"I think you probably know why I'm here."

He put his hands in his pockets as he took a couple of steps back from me. "Melissa."

"Good, I'm glad we aren't about to play a stupid game where you try to deny that you have no idea what is going on."

"Happy to be of assistance."

I leaned against the front door and folded my arms across my chest before I said, "You can assist me by leaving her alone."

"If she gives me what I want, then I will."

I unfolded my arms and stood up tall. "No can do."

"You're as stubborn as her, I see. Then tell her to give me what she stole from me, and she will be left out of anything that occurs after today."

"What the hell do you mean by that?" When he didn't answer, I continued. "Who are you working for? And we both know you're full of shit. You've never planned on leaving her alone even if she handed over the USB."

Calvin shrugged. "You might want to check in on your girl. Leaving her all alone couldn't have been a good choice to make. Wouldn't want to repeat history, am I right?"

It took less than a second for me to connect the dots. "If you lay a hand on her, I'm cutting yours off. You can call it an eye for an eye if you will."

I could read the fear coming from him in waves and that was good for me. If he touched her, he was a dead man, and I had no problem carrying that threat out myself. I stood up and walked toward the front door until I heard some shuffling behind me.

"Oh, Cross?"

I turned around and looked at Calvin, daring him to continue.

"Tell Kiki I said hello."

29

MELISSA

I was happy to have the opportunity to go get lunch with Nia today. Hanging out with her was my way of trying to stay connected with the friends I'd made since moving here. It had been a while since we saw each other in person anyway.

Nia rushed out from behind a clothing rack and said, "I'll be done in just a moment."

"Take your time," I said as I waved her off.

She rushed off in the opposite direction and I found some place to sit near the dressing room and pulled my phone out. At least I could distract myself with that until Nia was ready to go.

About five minutes passed and I heard someone sit close to me, but I didn't look up.

"Hello, Melissa. Long time no see."

I glanced to my right and caught myself before I gasped. "Kiki. Wasn't expecting to see you here. How are you?"

Although the way we met was unconventional, I told myself to keep things from becoming awkward.

"I'm well."

There was a pause in our conversation that forced an unsettling feeling to come between us. I put my phone down in my lap to look at her. I found her staring back at me and while I thought she was intimidating when I met her the first time, she had turned it up tenfold. But I refused to show that just her presence was affecting me.

"Listen," she said. "I wanted to warn you about something."

I raised an eyebrow at her. "And what is that?"

"Being involved with Gage is more trouble than it's worth."

This time, I couldn't control my emotions. How did she know anything about what Gage and I were doing? "What do you mean by that?"

"I'm telling you to get out while you're ahead. Being with him is only going to increase the likelihood of you getting hurt."

Kiki gathered the bags that she had placed at her feet and stood up. I thought her parting words might be something pleasant. I was wrong.

"You should ask your fuck buddy where you first had sex."

It was useless trying to contain my confusion. "What? I think I would know where I had sex with someone."

The wicked smile on her face said otherwise. "Have a good day, Melissa."

With that she walked away, and I sat there in silence as I tried to process what had just happened. I pulled out my phone and sent a text to Gage.

Me: *We need to talk. Just received a warning related to you.*

As I pressed send, Nia appeared. "I'm sorry that it took longer than I thought. Are you ready to go?"

I nodded as I stood up. "Yes. Let's go get something to eat."

～

WHEN WE ARRIVED AT LUNCH, things were awkward to say the least. Ever so often, I checked my phone to see if Gage had seen my message or responded and was disappointed to see he hadn't said anything yet. I tapped my fingers on my phone, trying to decide whether it was worth calling him or not. When Nia cleared her throat, my eyes flew to her.

"Are you okay? Your mind has been elsewhere since we arrived."

I pulled on my hair and said, "I'm sorry. Just dealing with a project at work and hoping that Gage will respond to me as soon as possible."

"I've been there, done that."

I was happy that she understood, but it didn't do much to ease my worry. One thing it did do was throw my appetite out the window. I couldn't dream of eating a thing right now.

"This might be a shitty thing to do, but could we postpone lunch? This project has me completely worried and I'm starting to feel nauseous."

Nia reached over and touched my hand. "Of course we can." She then looked around. "Let me see if I can find our server."

"Thank you and I'm sorry for being a shitty friend."

"It's not an issue. The next time we go to lunch or dinner, you owe me a drink." She shot me a sparkling smile.

I nodded. I had no problem with drinks being on me next time we went out.

Our server arrived and looked shocked that we were leaving. We reassured him that it had nothing to do with the service or food and that something had just come up and we needed to head out.

"Talk to me when you get back to the office okay?" Nia said when we were standing outside of the restaurant. "I'm worried about you."

"I will."

The car I called to pick me up arrived and I got in. There was no way I was going to be able to keep myself together if I took the subway. However, I rattled off my apartment address instead of Cross Industries because I couldn't go back to the office. I pulled out my phone and put a block on my calendar to show that I would be taking the rest of the day off. I also sent a quick message to Damien so that he didn't look for me.

When I opened my front door, I realized I still hadn't heard from Gage and my emotions were all over the place. They jumped between being worried about Gage to being angry about my run-in with Kiki. It wasn't until I walked over to my fridge to grab some water that my phone rang, and I almost sprained my ankle trying to get to it.

"Gage?"

"I'm leaving the airport now and I'll be at your place soon."

～

MY LEG JITTERED as I sat on my couch, waiting for Gage to come to my apartment. I knew that he had landed and would arrive sooner rather than later, and with that news, my nerves were a mess. I was on the verge of feeling sick, but I needed to see this through. I didn't trust Kiki as far as I could throw her, but it was clear that I was in the dark about something, but what exactly I didn't know.

When my phone rang, I immediately grabbed it and answered without a second thought. "Are you here?"

"Yes." The anxiousness in his voice was easy to pick up on and it wasn't something I was used to hearing from him.

"Okay I'll come down."

I hung up, grabbed my keys, and dashed downstairs. I could have stayed and waited for him to come to me, but I was too worried. I had no idea if I should be happy or angry about seeing him, but my heart skipped a beat after not seeing him for seventy-two hours. He looked as handsome as ever even if his clothes were disheveled. The scruff on his face made him look even more dangerous but the slight circles under his eyes had me worried.

Gage pulled me into his arms and held me for what felt like an eternity. I was glad to be back in his arms, but my heart cracked a bit given how long he was hanging on. The strength and confidence that he usually exhibited was nowhere to be found.

Instead of saying anything, I grabbed his hand and together we walked up to my apartment. Once I closed the door behind us, I found him sitting on my couch. Neither one of us had said a word since he'd called me and that needed to end.

"Can I get you anything?"

Gage shook his head but said nothing.

"I assume your work trip didn't go well."

"It wasn't a work trip."

So, he'd lied about that. Awesome. That didn't make me feel great about how this conversation was going to go.

"Why did you lie about it? What type of trip was it?"

He still hadn't looked at me since he'd entered the apartment, something I found troublesome and did little to make me feel as if everything was going to be fine.

"I didn't want you to know that I was visiting Calvin."

I gasped and grabbed his hand. "You went and saw him without telling me? The issue that I have with him has nothing to do with you."

"I told you I was going to take care of it." Gage sighed and then added, "I need to tell you about something."

I frowned. "What?" I asked warily.

"I've been doing research into Kiki Hastings."

"Why and what does she have to do with Calvin?"

"I'm getting to that." Gage took a breath, and I knew what he was about to say would change everything. "When I was sixteen, Kiki tried to seduce me, my dad caught her, and you can imagine what happened. She's an abuser, however she's managed to get away with it forever. I'm trying to put a stop to her."

"Gage, I didn't know… that must have been—"

"Stop, it was fine, nothing serious happened, at least not to me. But to others I know…" Gage nodded then looked away. "When I saw Calvin, he said, 'Say hello to Kiki for me.' Then you sent that text."

"Wait, you need to realize that what she did to you was still sexual abuse."

"I know that…now."

"I don't understand. How did Calvin know about Kiki?"

"I don't know. Something connects them, but I'm not sure what yet. In any case, I can guess who gave you that warning about me. Kiki."

I nodded.

"About eight months ago, I went looking into Kiki, as I said. She happened to be having a party that night."

He pulled something out of his pocket and tossed it between the two of us. I picked it up and realized it was a mask; the same mask that the person who I'd met at Kiki's party had worn. Bile rose in my mouth as my thoughts raced and I started connecting the dots. I'd noticed that some things were familiar but didn't know it was him. Anger replaced the feelings of hurt that coursed through me.

"When did you find out who I was?"

"Sweetheart, I—"

"My name is Melissa. Can you stop lying for once? When. Did. You. Find. Out?"

"Soon after you became my assistant."

I swore, feeling as if I'd been completely blind to something that was staring me right in the face.

"How could you do this to me? I thought, I thought we had something, but clearly I was wrong."

"I know how it seems, but it's not like that—"

"Just shut up, Gage! I can't believe I ever trusted you!"

"Sweetheart, wait," Gage started.

"No! Get out! Get out of my apartment! Now!" Tears gathered around the edges of my eyes, but I wouldn't let them fall, not yet. Not till he was gone.

Gage looked at me, then shook his head and strode out, slamming my door behind himself, as if he were the wronged party here.

As his footsteps faded, I let the tears fall. My heart was breaking as I sat down on the couch. I felt bad about what he admitted to me had happened with Kiki, but I was in too much pain because of the betrayal I felt.

I should have known better than to get involved with Gage Cross.

30

MELISSA

My office phone rang, and I did a double take when I saw whose name popped up on the caller ID. I took a deep breath to steady my heart and answered.

"Hello, Mr. Cross."

"Hi, Melissa. I was wondering if you were available to meet with me in my office?"

"Sure. What time works best for you?"

"Right now."

There would be no time to prepare for this. "Okay I'll head up now. Do I need to bring anything with me?"

"Excellent. No, you don't."

With that he hung up and I placed the phone back down on the hook. I grabbed the edge of my desk, willing my heart to stop racing.

It was my first day back at the office after taking a couple days off because of how I felt after Gage's betrayal. Although it still hurt, it took some time for me to admit that I missed him, but wasn't ready to speak to him yet. What I had been planning on doing was trying my best to dodge Gage, but he hadn't appeared this morning. What I wasn't planning on doing was having Mr. Cross call me and ask me to meet with him in his office.

I stood up on shaky knees and was reminded of the reaction I had when Mr. Cross had sent me the email that then led to me finding out about the promotion I was going to get. Maybe this meeting had something to do with that?

I was determined to keep the thoughts swirling in my head positive as I walked to the elevator and took it to the top floor.

Ellen welcomed me with a warm smile. "Go right in, he's waiting on you."

I gave her a small smile in return and walked right past her. I knocked on his open door and Martin Cross looked up and directly at me.

"Melissa."

"Yes, sir." I didn't recognize my own voice as my heart leapt into my throat, the possibilities of why he could want me to come see him running through my mind.

"Please close the door and take a seat. There is something we need to talk about."

Without another word, I closed the door and sat down in the chair in front of his desk and waited patiently for him to continue.

"There are some things we need to discuss before we talk about transitioning you to your new position."

My heart slowly dislodged from my throat, and I began to breathe again. "Yes?"

"Both Gage and Damien have spoken very highly of you, and I appreciate your tenacity in what I assume was a hellish few weeks while you were working for both of them."

I nodded. "Yes, but it was worth it. Not only was I able to learn things from both positions, it showed me that I could take on more than I thought I could and continue to thrive."

I felt as if I was selling myself to him even though he said that I had the new position. If I wasn't so nervous, I probably would have laughed at the double entendre I made about being able to learn things from Gage because that extended far beyond the boardroom.

"I say all this because I would completely understand if you decided not to take this position given what I'm about to tell you."

"Wait, what?" Here was the second member of the Cross family who had been hiding something from me.

"I'm not going to insult your intelligence and ask you if you know Linda St. Hill."

"Of course I do. That's my mother."

"Well, I knew her. Quite well actually. We went to college together."

I forced my brain to try to piece together this new development. "You went to Brentson University. My mom went to—"

"She was a couple of years older than me and transferred back to a college in Ohio. She and I kept in touch over the years every so often, and when she knew that you had gotten into NYU, she asked if I would keep an eye on you while you were there."

"But I never met you until—" I stopped as all my thoughts came crashing down in my mind. I recalled what had happened on one of my last days of college. "The job as

Damien's assistant didn't just fall out of the sky and land on my college career counselor's lap. You made sure I knew about it."

"That is true."

I couldn't control my anger. I'd once again been manipulated by someone else in the span of a week. Another person had removed my right to choose.

"Why did you wait until now to tell me? Is this promotion something else that you're just giving me?" I couldn't look him in the eye because I was so angry. My voice was low, almost raspy, and I clenched my fists, trying to do everything I could do to remain calm. I tried to remind myself over and over again that this job had afforded me all of the luxuries I currently had and that it was best to keep my cool until I could think straight.

For a second, Mr. Cross looked shocked that I would say that. "Nothing was given to you. We didn't hire you because I knew your mother. We hired you because we knew you were qualified for the job and that investing our resources in you would be beneficial for both you and the company. If you weren't a good fit for here, we would have found a way so that you landed on your feet somewhere else. But I wanted you to know this so that if you did take the management position, you knew that it had nothing to do with anything outside of your own merit and the work you put in since the day you walked through Cross Industries' front doors."

I wanted to believe it was true, but I couldn't shake the news that he had just told me and the fact that I'd been sleeping with a man that was considered to be my boss up until just a few nights ago.

"All that is to say that the management position is yours if you choose to take it. We can start the transition as soon as you're ready."

"Do I have a deadline to let you know whether or not I will be taking the position?"

It was Mr. Cross's turn to look taken aback. I'm sure in all of his years of running this empire, very few people had questioned whether or not they wanted a position at Cross Industries, let alone a promotion. "You'll have a couple of days."

I stood up, considering this the end of the conversation. "Well, it's clear that I have a lot of things to think about."

"That you do."

I turned and walked toward his office door. My hand was on the doorknob when I heard Mr. Cross call my name again.

"I wouldn't change anything I did because I kept my promise to your mother."

"I know."

31

GAGE

I grunted as I exerted more energy than I intended to, but it felt good to work out. I deemed it better than staying in my apartment and sulking, wondering whether it would be a disservice to myself to pour another glass of whatever liquor I could find to drown my feelings. The last few days without Melissa had been hell.

"I was shocked when you told me that you were in the gym."

I didn't bother to turn around to find my father standing behind me. After all, I knew he was coming to see me.

"Haven't seen you around the office lately."

I stopped my bicep curl and looked over at him. "We rarely see each other anyway. Busy schedules and all of that."

With a heavy breath my father took a couple of steps toward me. "I didn't come here to start anything."

"Then why'd you come?"

"Partially to talk some sense into you."

I grunted again, but it had nothing to do with my workout. I wasn't happy about where this conversation was going. "About what?"

"There's something else you should know."

The way he said it made me turn around. "What happened?"

He put one hand in his pocket before he told me everything about how he'd made a promise to Melissa's mother to help when he could and how that led to her applying for a job.

"You never mentioned this."

"Didn't think it mattered...until you fell in love with her."

I stood perfectly still for a beat. "Dad, you must be—"

"Gage, I heard that you took her to Elevate with you for the anniversary party and surprised her with a work conference trip. I know she does great work and I'm sure she was helpful, but I thought it was suspicious since you've never done anything like that before."

"I could have been turning over a new leaf."

Dad could read my bullshit from a mile away and didn't look impressed.

"Just because you haven't admitted it to yourself yet doesn't mean it isn't true. You wouldn't be avoiding her like you are if you didn't. You're afraid to see the damage you've done to her. And based on what I've seen, it's quite severe."

"I didn't ask." I went back to starting another set of bicep curls.

"When you take your head out of your own ass, go and fix things with her. After all, she's no longer your assistant."

That forced me to stop again, and I found myself staring into my father's eyes. I knew he was about to call my bluff and there was nothing I could do to prevent it. "Everything went through with her promotion?"

"It has and if she wants the job, it's hers."

I decided there was no use in trying to hide it now. "What do you mean if she wants it? Of course she wants it."

My father shook his head. "I understand why she's hesitant to take the job now. She didn't have much of a choice in how things came to be and if she wants to switch things up so she can find her own way, she should have the right to do so. Anyway, I'll leave you to finish your workout. I hope this at least gave you something to think about."

Dad lingered for a moment before breaking eye contact and turning away. I refused to think about anything related to Melissa until I wrapped up this workout and headed upstairs.

It took no time before I was freshly showered and sitting at my kitchen counter, mindlessly scrolling on my phone. I thought about calling Kingston to see if there was anything I could help him with but that would be pointless. I was too distracted by what my father had said when he stopped by. It made me reflect again on how I'd deceived Melissa by not telling her when we first met; part of it was out of fear of what she would think and how that would affect getting her into my bed. That had been the objective.

Making sure that she ended up in my bed for however long I wanted her there.

And now that all had changed. All of this could have been prevented if I'd just been straight with her. Explained how I hadn't known who she was that night, but later figured it out. How I shouldn't have taken advantage of the situation.

I couldn't pinpoint exactly when our relationship had

evolved into something I wasn't expecting, but there was no denying that it had. And I missed her terribly.

Dad was right and I hadn't wanted to admit it to myself. But usually when someone else tells you something, you listen.

I didn't know the first step I should take outside of apologizing and risking her slamming a door in my face. As I stood up, I heard something that caused me to pause.

Someone was at the front door, trying to get in.

I sprinted into action and reached for a gun that I kept in one of my barely used kitchen cabinets.

When my front door lock disengaged, I was there to greet them with a gun pointed at their face.

"Gage."

"I could have shot you. Why didn't you tell me you were coming by?"

"Because I didn't have much time and you gave me a key that I couldn't find right away. We need to go. Now."

"Why?"

"I was about to come up to talk to you and decided to check in on the cameras that we installed at Melissa's place. Calvin just showed up."

32

MELISSA

I entered my apartment, carrying the groceries I'd purchased over the threshold without too much trouble. I closed the front door and turned on the light near it and screamed.

Calvin was sitting on my couch, staring back at me with an amused look on his face.

"Welcome home, Melissa. Now it seems that you are quite busy, so I want to get out of your hair as quickly as possible. Give me the USB."

I was still processing that I wasn't alone and that my worst fears had come true. Deep down, I knew it was only a matter of time. I hadn't been that hard to find and I ran into him at the work conference that Gage and I attended together. Although I was pissed at Gage for not telling me where he was going when he visited Calvin, I'd hoped that the confrontation would have put a stop to an event like this from occurring. Clearly, I was wrong.

"Where is what? I have no idea what you're talking about."

"Don't play stupid with me, little girl. The last thing you want to do is piss me off."

His demeaning words and tone did little to alter the frostiness in my own voice. "I'm not giving you a thing and you can go to fucking hell."

"Still stubborn, eh? I have ways that can make you change your mind quickly."

"What you can do is leave my home immediately. If you don't, you'll regret it."

He stood up and his imposing body told me that I more than likely wasn't going to win this by attacking him head-on with no weapon. He had at least eight inches on me and probably seventy-five pounds. But I had an advantage that he didn't. I knew the space very well, including where I kept another can of mace. It, along with several knives, was in the kitchen, but my main concern was how I was going to get around him. Getting out of this alive was the main objective because I knew that he had no problem killing me right where I stood. The only thing probably keeping me alive was the fact that I knew where the USB was and would save Calvin a ton of time if he could get its location out of me instead of having to search for it himself.

He took his time removing a gun from a holster that I hadn't noticed he was carrying. He toyed with the gun before pointing it at me. A shiver went down my spine as I swallowed hard. "What, is someone supposed to be coming for you? The detail that was watching over you is long gone now."

He'd had someone watching outside of my building? But if what Calvin was saying was true, then the likelihood of someone coming to help me had diminished. I was on my own and had to figure out a way out of this. Much like I always had to.

"That was by design. I know it was you that kept calling me."

He shrugged. "I was doing what I had to do to get what belongs to me. And now you are trying my patience. Where is it?"

I sat back with a confused look on my face.

That was a lie. I knew exactly what he was talking about, but I wasn't about to give up my insurance policy. I was worried about this happening at all but having it happen in my apartment was problematic. There was a high chance that he would hurt me and if he did, there were no witnesses.

A knock on the door forced the air in my lungs to leave in a rush. Could it be someone who might be able to save my life? When a grin appeared on his lips, I knew that that wasn't the case.

"Door's open," he said, and I waited to see who would be joining this reunion.

I did a double take when Kiki entered the room. What the hell did she have to do with this?

"Surprised to see me?"

"You could say that."

"I warned you that being with Gage could mean trouble for you and then he just had to go and pay Calvin a visit. What's interesting now is that since you two have broken up, it made it even easier to track you."

"So in reality, I did what you said, and I'm still being punished. Interesting."

Kiki flipped her hair over her shoulder. "I never said that the world was fair. Now hand it over."

A dry chuckle left my lips. I had nothing left to lose because I was going to die either way. "Do you think that just because you asked this time, and he didn't that I was going to hand it over? Fuck you both."

"You're just as stupid and dumb as your mother and Hayley Cross."

The statement puzzled me and threw me off my game and I briefly let my guard down. Kiki took advantage of it and swiftly walked over to me and yanked me by my hair. I hissed in response.

"Tell us where it is."

Instead of responding, I let instinct take over and spit in her face. That caused a chain reaction that I'd been waiting for.

Kiki screamed in shock, which seemed to surprise Calvin because he fired a shot. It was clear that he wasn't used to handling this type of business because he wasn't prepared. Instead of watching Kiki, I charged at him, throwing all of my weight at him. I knew there was no way that I would be able to overpower him and her at the same time, but if I could use the strengths that I had to my advantage, maybe I had a chance.

He threw me off of him, stunning me for a moment. It took me a second to gather my bearings before I sprinted to the kitchen. Just as I was about to grab one of my knives, something heavy hit me in the back, causing me to fall to the floor.

Pain radiated through my body as I tried to get back up and it took everything in me to turn my body around so I could face my assailant.

"You just couldn't do what you're told, could you?"

It took a bit to focus on Calvin due to the pain I was feeling. An evil smile crossed his face and made me want to cry. It could have been as a result of the shooting pain that was flying through my body that was also contributing to the tears pooling in the corners of my eyes.

Once I had a clear image of him, I said, "I've weighed my options and am prepared to die if necessary. There's no way I'm handing it over to you."

"I have to admit that I admire your bravery even if it is stupid."

"Wouldn't be the first time I heard that."

The front door burst open once more and I gasped. I watched as Gage's eyes flew around the room, assessing the situation before they landed on me. Before I could comprehend what was going on, he aimed his gun at Calvin.

"Put the gun down. It won't be worth ruining that pristine suit you have on there."

"Gage, I think it is you who should put their gun down. After all, I have no problem shooting her and taking her down with me."

"That wouldn't be wise."

Calvin glanced to the doorway where Gage and Kingston stood and smiled at me. "It's been a while, Kingston. How are things?"

"Peachy," Kingston replied. He and Gage walked farther into the room as I heard my heart pounding in my ears. He too aimed his gun at Calvin. "End this now by putting your gun down."

"Or what? You're going to kill me? Sounds great because I have nothing left to lose because of this bitch."

That was all it took. A shot fired off and I screamed in

disbelief. I watched as Calvin stiffened before crumbling to the ground. There was more commotion before I spotted Gage in front of me.

I couldn't stop my body from trembling after what had just occurred. Were my eyes playing tricks on me? Gage had murdered someone in hopes of saving my life.

"Are you okay?" His eyes focused on what I knew had to be a nice-sized gash on my head.

"My head is pounding and my back hurts, but other than that I'm fine."

He pulled me into his arms and just held me, making sure not to further irritate any of my injuries.

"It's going to be okay," he said as he gently held my hair, rocking me back and forth. I didn't know how long we sat like that when I heard Gage ask, "Where is Kiki?"

I pulled away from him and looked around to see where she was.

"Let her go."

Gage and I looked at Kingston and I wondered if he had lost his mind. Gage spoke for both of us. "What do you mean—"

"I said I let Kiki go. We'll take care of that later."

The seriousness in Kingston's voice must have been enough to convince Gage not to say any more. Instead, he pulled me into his arms again.

When Kingston came into view, I lifted my head from where it was resting on Gage's chest and said, "Kiki mentioned something about a Hayley Cross. Who is that?"

Gage and Kingston shared a look before Kingston's face hardened. "My dead wife."

33

GAGE

I continued to brush Melissa's curls with my hand as she cuddled up with me on my couch. After what had turned into a long evening, it felt good to have her back in my home and in my arms.

There wasn't much we could do to hide this from the police due to how loud everything had been, and we'd all spent a long time running through our story, which was easy to keep straight because most of what we said was true. There was a chance that charges might get brought up due to me shooting and killing Calvin, but we'd deal with that when it came to it. Plus, we had evidence of how he'd been harassing Melissa. In my opinion, the end justified the means. Melissa was safe and Calvin wouldn't bother her again. Hell, even Kiki wasn't on my radar now because of Kingston's reassurance that it would all be taken care of. There was one person who I was still concerned about.

My cheek grazed Melissa's hair before I bent down and kissed the top of her head. "It's over," I whispered to her. I was determined that she wouldn't have to worry about anything related to this ever again.

"Is it? Because it sure doesn't feel like it."

"It is because I won't let him hurt you ever again. I'm sorry for all the pain he has caused you. Hell, I'm sorry for all of the pain that I've caused you."

I looked down at her before I continued, "I love you. If that wasn't already apparent."

"It was."

She moved her head to look at me and we both burst out laughing. Her laughter was like music to my ears, something I'd longed to hear for what felt like so long and had missed.

"Don't you have something to say back to me?"

"Cocky much?"

"Because I can back it up. And once you're feeling better, I'll remind you."

"Can't wait."

She shifted her body so that she could lean up and kiss me, but before her lips landed on mine, she whispered, "I love you."

"Gage?"

Kingston walked over to me where I was standing looking out the window, lost in my thoughts. Melissa had gone to bed what seemed like hours ago and Kingston and I stayed awake trying to figure out our next steps. "What?"

"You need to head out."

"Why's that? And where am I going?"

Kingston patted me on the back. "I'm not sure why you've

been fixated on Kiki Hastings, but it's time to end this. I've sent you the address of where you're supposed to go."

I checked my phone and saw that he had sent me a link. When I clicked it, my GPS app opened, and I skimmed the directions as he continued. "You can take my SUV. I'll stay here with Melissa in case she wakes up."

I nodded as he handed me the keys. I knew what he meant by ending this tonight and I was glad that I wouldn't have to wait too long now to enact my revenge. I walked over to my bedroom door and slowly opened it. I saw that Melissa was resting peacefully and I knew I would carry out what would hopefully be the last task of this hellish couple of weeks.

It was easy to find Kingston's SUV because he was the one that drove us back to my place. I hooked up my phone to the dashboard and set my GPS to start telling me directions and off I was. The journey out of the city didn't take long and I wasn't surprised by how rural things had become. Based on the map that I saw when Kingston sent me the link, I knew he wasn't directing me to the place where Cross Sentinel had a warehouse in Staten Island, but it had the same rural feel. As I drove through the night, all I could do was play the events that occurred over the last few hours on repeat in my mind. The fear I felt for Melissa, killing Calvin, and being pissed that Kiki got away. It wasn't until I got closer to the location that I was able to turn my emotions off and focus on whatever the rest of the night was going to bring me.

When I reached the location that my GPS told me was where I was supposed to be, my headlights landed on a car. Before I could turn my headlights off, someone stepped out of the driver's side door, and I did a double take when I recognized Ace Bolton.

"What are you doing here?"

"I got called to deliver this special package." He used his thumb to point back at the car. That was when I saw a figure in the backseat. Thankfully I'd forgotten to turn off my headlights because it was easy to recognize Kiki in the backseat.

I opened the door and was smacked in the face with the smell of gasoline. I knew my time with her was limited.

"Who greased some hands so that the charges against you were dropped?"

Kiki smiled. "What's the point in telling you? It's not like it's going to save my life anyway. Martin and Selena tried to make my life a living hell years ago after they kicked me out of their inner circle, but I preserved. I already got what I wanted: I made it so that you'll never forget me."

"You are sick. Even as you're about to die, you can't in your good conscience do something right. Ace?"

"Yea?"

"Do you have anything that you want to say to her?"

He shook his head. "She and I had plenty to talk about on the way here."

"Then, you do the honors." I rolled down the window a bit and then slammed the door of the car shut. Hopefully that crack in the window would allow some of the air to get out so she wouldn't die from smoke inhalation, but from the burns of the fire as it pierced her skin.

"The answer is closer than you think."

She'd barely got the words out before the fire in the car started getting to her and all Ace and I could hear were her screams. He and I stood there watching as the car burned and he pulled something out of his pocket to hand to me.

"Cigarette?"

"Nah, man I don't smoke."

He looked at me, then at the cigarettes, and then back at me. "Yeah, I probably shouldn't either."

EPILOGUE
GAGE

Dad looked between me and Melissa, questions in his eyes. "I'm happy you're back together, but..."

We were back in the office about two weeks later and I'd convinced Melissa to attend this meeting because I knew what it would be about. She was about two weeks out from starting her new management position and had taken some time off before the transition. She'd been staying with me since the night we said I love you to one another and we'd both came into the office together. "She's here because I'm not letting her out of my sight. At least not for a long time."

"That's understandable." He looked at each of his sons and his nephew before turning to look at Melissa. Although her face was looking a lot better, some of the injuries were still visible. Melissa had also been taking care of the injuries that weren't visible to the naked eye and had been seeking therapy to work through some of the issues she'd faced due to Calvin coming after her and from her mother's death at a young age. I'd been there supporting her every step of the way and, as a result, we'd grown closer together. With all of the things that had happened, I wouldn't change much of it outside of the pain that Melissa had to endure because it had made us a stronger couple in the process.

Damien looked at Melissa and me before he spoke. "So, both threats have been eliminated. But I don't think that this is the end. Not by a long shot."

Broderick stroked his chin and said, "No, because I can't see Vincent, Kiki, Calvin and Malcom being connected. Specifically, Kiki would probably think Vincent was scum of the Earth after he got banished from the Vitale family."

I nodded because it was a good point. "Who would have the means to pull all of this together, including digging into Melissa's background to find someone to terrorize her from her past? I'm sure the answer to who is coming after us is in Kiki's little black book," I offered. "How do we get it since she's now dead?"

"There's no need to look in there."

We turned toward my father and I pulled Melissa closer to me although I knew the voice like I knew my own.

Dad.

Damien spoke up first. "What are you talking about?"

"I think you need to take a deeper look at someone closer to us."

Broderick took a step closer to our father and crossed his arms. The question floating in the room was apparent and I was eagerly awaiting my father's response.

I trusted everyone in this room with my life so there was no doubt in my mind that it wasn't anyone here.

Yet, I still hadn't been expecting Dad's answer. "My brother."

All eyes shifted from Dad to my cousin, who we all knew had suffered a great loss that we now knew was at the hands of his father. Nothing on his face alluded to what he was thinking, but it wouldn't take much to guess what he was feeling.

"Are you going to tell us how you know?" Broderick asked.

Before Dad could continue, Damien took a step toward Kingston, who shook his head once, essentially warning him not to come any closer. His gaze shifted to each of us, one by one, and when his eyes landed on me, I was able to read his mind. I nodded slightly and he walked out of the room, revenge flashing in his eyes.

∼

THANK you for reading Secret Empire! While Melissa and Gage's story is complete, the Broken Cross series continues with Stolen Empire, Kingston and Ellie's book. Keep reading to find a sneak peek of it!

DON'T WANT to let Melissa and Gage go just yet? Click HERE to grab a bonus scene featuring the couple!

WANT to join discussions about the Broken Cross Series? Click HERE to join my Reader Group on Facebook.

PLEASE JOIN my newsletter to find out the latest about the Broken Cross series and my other books!

STOLEN EMPIRE BLURB

What was stolen…

When my world was ripped out from under me,
    I craved solitude so that I could heal.
    It became a habit until I saw her.
    She might hate me,
    But that's okay.
    She doesn't know that she's my obsession.
    And I'm the only one who can protect her,
    Because she's mine.

SNEAK PEEK AT STOLEN EMPIRE
KINGSTON

My father.

That was all I could think of as I watched the water gently sway around my ankles. I'd probably suspected everyone around me at one point or another while grieving and showcased my anger in numerous ways.

I'd failed to protect her.

I remembered it feeling as if my sanity was on the brink and could snap at any second.

In the days since her death, I remember Damien coming to me and trying to be a sounding board because he too knew what it was like to lose someone, even if Charlotte wasn't dead.

Although she'd died years ago now, there was still unfinished business that I felt I needed to take care of, and now I knew it involved the person who was supposed to always be in my corner no matter what.

Not that that meant anything. He'd never had my back when I was growing up, so why would he start now?

That didn't mean that I thought he would kill my wife.

I'd kept my distance from my family for a while, including my mother, who had tried to be a beacon of light during my darkest days. But it wasn't enough. I needed to be by myself to heal.

Heal? That was almost comical because I still couldn't tell anyone if I was healed today.

It'd been seven long years of pain, sacrifice, and anger. Anger about why I couldn't have stopped it from happening.

And the kicker was that my father had organized it all.

He didn't care how much turmoil he caused or what devastation he left in his wake. All that mattered was him getting what he wanted, no matter the cost.

Well, payback is a bitch, and he should have known that as soon as he did what he did, that I would be coming after him and I wouldn't stop until I achieved my goal: having his head on a platter.

A lot of the puzzle pieces were falling into place. If Uncle Martin knew that my father was responsible for the death of my wife and for trying to cause harm to my cousins, I knew it was because he wanted us to know. But what else he had up his sleeve would be anyone's guess and I would do everything to protect anything that was mine.

That meant Ellie Winters.

My obsession.

My soon-to-be everything.

Stolen Empire is available for pre-order and will be released in fall 2021.

ABOUT THE AUTHOR

Bri loves a good romance, especially ones that involve a hot anti-hero. That is why she likes to turn the dial up a notch with her own writing. Her Broken Cross series is her debut dark romance series.

She spends most of her time hanging out with her family, plotting her next novel, or reading books by other romance authors.

briblackwood.com

ALSO BY BRI BLACKWOOD

Broken Cross Series

Sinners Empire (Prequel)

Savage Empire

Scarred Empire

Steel Empire

Shadow Empire

Secret Empire

Stolen Empire

Brentson University Series

Devious Game

Made in United States
Cleveland, OH
30 December 2024